ARCH-
CONSPIRATOR

Also by VERONICA ROTH

Chosen Ones

Poster Girl

ARCH-
CONSPIRATOR

VERONICA
ROTH

TOR

TOR PUBLISHING GROUP
NEW YORK

ARCH-CONSPIRATOR

A Tor Book
Published by Tom Doherty Associates / Tor Publishing Group
120 Broadway
New York, NY 10271

www.tor-forge.com

Tor® is a registered trademark of Macmillan Publishing Group, LLC.

Library of Congress Cataloging-in-Publication Data

Names: Roth, Veronica, author.
Title: Arch-conspirator / Veronica Roth.
Description: First Edition. | New York : Tor, 2023. | "A Tor Publishing Group Book."
Identifiers: LCCN 2022034350 (print) | LCCN 2022034351 (ebook) | ISBN 9781250855466 (hardcover) | ISBN 9781250889515 (signed edition) | ISBN 9781250855473 (ebook)
Subjects: LCGFT: Novels.
Classification: LCC PS3618.O8633 A73 2023 (print) | LCC PS3618.O8633 (ebook) | DDC 813/.6—dc23/eng/20220722
LC record available at https://lccn.loc.gov/2022034350
LC ebook record available at https://lccn.loc.gov/2022034351

Our books may be purchased in bulk for promotional, educational, or business use. Please contact your local bookseller or the Macmillan Corporate and Premium Sales Department at 1-800-221-7945, extension 5442, or by email at MacmillanSpecialMarkets@macmillan.com.

First Edition: 2023

Printed in the United States of America

0 9 8 7 6 5 4 3 2 1

To all the teachers over the years
who taught me how to read thoughtfully

But though she be my sister's child or nearer
Of kin than all who worship at my hearth,
Nor she nor yet her sister shall escape
The utmost penalty, for both I hold,
As arch-conspirators, of equal guilt.
—Sophocles, *Antigone*

ARCH-
CONSPIRATOR

1

Antigone

I asked my father, once, why he chose to curse us before we were born. Because to be born as my siblings and I were was to be doomed from the start. We were unique among our people, pieced together from whatever random combination of genes our two parents provided. Table-scrap children.

He didn't say, as my mother had, a year before, "We didn't think it was a curse."

He was far too unsentimental for that.

"We thought," he said to me, "it was a curse worth bearing."

An honest man, and now a dead one.

He was in the courtyard, the man who killed my father. Oh, perhaps he hadn't held the blade, but the coup that wrenched political power from my father's hands and then trampled him beneath its boots was Kreon's coup, undergone for Kreon, by Kreon.

He was in the casual version of his uniform, pants tucked into boots, shirt tucked into pants, forehead dotted with sweat, the morning sun already applying pressure. He bent his head to listen to the head of his guard, Nikias. They were too far away for me to hear.

I was on a balcony, nestled in ivy that grew only here, in the High Commander's courtyard, where no amount of water scarcity in other parts of the city could convince Kreon to sacrifice beauty. *People will permit a High Commander his small indulgences,* I had heard him say once. *It is such a difficult job.*

I imagined he was right—it was a difficult job, keeping a tight fist for so long. But I wasn't sure any amount of ivy could make this place beautiful to me.

Nikias moved away from Kreon, no doubt sent on some small mission. My uncle's eyes lifted to mine. He nodded in greeting.

My throat tightened. I disappeared into the leaves.

After the fighting had ceased, after we had found our father and mother's bodies in the streets, washed them, prayed over them; after I had Extracted their ichor, too young for the responsibility and yet the only ones to do it; after we had stored what was left of them in the Archive; after all that, Kreon had summoned us to this house, to that courtyard where the ivy grew and the street spilled in, and, in the presence of all who had ears to hear, told us we were welcome to live with him there. To this day, I'm not sure what prompted this act of generosity. We disgust Kreon, as we disgust many in this city, because of our origins.

Perhaps it was because we were family, and there were rules for family, and Kreon loved rules. Kreon was Oedipus's brother, Oedipus's shadow. A man of the blade instead of a man of the mind. At family gatherings when I was young, he was known for breaking things—glasses, plates, toys—just from handling them too roughly. Once, my mother asked him to brush Ismene's hair for her, and Ismene spent the entire time trying not to cry as he ripped knots out of her head. He didn't know how to be teased; he only laughed at other people, never himself.

Perhaps it wasn't because we were family—perhaps it was because we were children of *Oedipus*, warped though we were by our genes. And Oedipus had almost started a revolution—he was a symbol, and so were we. And what better way to take the power from a symbol than to claim it as your own?

So when Kreon told us we were welcome to live in his house, I knew what the consequences would be: he would let Polyneikes and Eteocles and Ismene and me live, but we would do so at his pleasure. We would live in his house, lending legitimacy to his rule, and he would keep his eye on us.

We thank you for your generosity, I had told him, in the moment.

2

Polyneikes

Been coming here to the Cafe Athena for several years now, ever since I had spend to burn and *she* started working here. It was her dad's shop—had to be, or she wouldn't have been working—but mostly he wasn't there to catch me staring. Figured every woman, from the first one who ever gave me that funny feeling to the one I ultimately got assigned to, would be doing the same equation: add my famous parents, tragic backstory, generational wealth, and winsome smile, and subtract the unsettling reality of my busted genetic code, and what do you get? Someone worth messing around with?

If the waitress at the Athena even bothered with the calculus, she came up decidedly "not interested," but the coffee tasted less burnt here than in most other places, so I kept coming anyhow.

"This isn't coffee," Parth said to me after his first sip. "It's liquid shit."

True, it wasn't coffee—there were just a handful of coffee plants in the greenhouses, so only a lucky few had ever had the real stuff. This was just an approximation of coffee, with a conjecture of sugar stirred into it.

I was sitting at the least rickety of the tables out front, street-side, my toe wedged under one of the table legs to steady it. The seat across from me was empty, but Parth was standing, drinking from a tiny mug that made his hand look comically large. Somebody pedaled past with a bucket of paper flowers hanging off the back of her bicycle; one of them toppled onto the stones. Nabbed right away by a beggar kid with a cup for coin. He stuck it behind his ear.

"You could sit," I said to Parth. "Tig probably won't be on time."

"These chairs make me feel like I'm playing teatime with my niece," he said. Big guy, Parth was. Had the look of a guy who would turn out to be a softie, only he wasn't. Too tricky for that. "Plus, I'm done. You let her come all the way here by herself? Some brother."

"Tig can handle herself."

Parth set his mini mug down on the table and eyed me. "You're not gonna tell her nothing, right?"

"Of course not. But you know her, she might figure it out anyway."

"Just so long as she doesn't interfere."

"Interfere with what?" a slim, reedy voice asked from behind him. And there she was: my sister, sidling up just as the clock struck 1400 hours.

"Antigone," Parth said to her, with a head bob that was supposed to be like a bow.

"Parthenopaeus," she replied. "Will you be joining us?"

"No, gotta run," he said. "See you later, Pol."

He dodged the beggar kid and his cup, crossed the street, and disappeared into a crooked alley. A gust of wind came up behind him, blowing dust into the air. Antigone pulled the scarf she wore over her hair across her nose and mouth until it settled. I just held my breath.

The waitress came by, that little bounce in her walk, and brought two cups of coffee, black, and a pile of sweetener cubes stacked neat like a temple. She didn't look either of us in the eye. Didn't ask if we'd like anything else.

"Thought you liked the service here," Antigone said.

"I like the look of it."

She snorted. "You don't care who treats you like a pariah, as long as she's got nice legs?"

"Can't fault people for learning what they're taught."

"Can, too. I do it all the time," she said. "So what was Parth on about?"

Should have known she wouldn't let that go.

"Something's brewing," I said. "You know that."

"Something's *been* brewing," she said. "You could just tell me what's going on."

"No need," I said. "No help necessary, and it would just put you in a bad spot."

She frowned at me. Back when we were kids, we went in and out of looking like our parents. Dad said kids were like that, mushy, sculptures still drying in the sun. Now, though, Tig was settled, hardened, and she looked just like Mom. Bend at the bridge of her nose, weak chin, big round eyes.

"I'm already in a bad spot," she said, sharp as noon sun. "I live in the house of my patricide, and I'm betrothed to his son."

"Yeah, but there's a difference between a bad spot I put you in and a bad spot I didn't," I said. "Plus, the others would kill me. No potential mothers allowed at this level of the operation, you know that."

"Ah, yes." Sour as, and *this* is nothing like our mom, who could rip you to shreds with a gentle word, if she chose. No subtle streak in Antigone; she's more like Dad in that way. "Can't risk me; I'm just a viable womb on stilts."

"That is the general attitude."

"Fuck, Pol," she said, leaning over the table, her scarf almost falling into her coffee. "I'm so tired of that."

We both looked across at the little shop with its wares spilling out into the street. Stacks of old cookware, tangles of wires, piles of light bulbs still in their boxes, a rack of sunglasses with mostly intact lenses.

"It's not me, though." I reached across the table and covered her hand where it clasped the mug. "You know that, right? I know everything would be better if you were involved. It's just that we're trying to unite seven districts, and some of them are more . . . *traditional* than others. We're only as strong as our weakest links."

Her hand trembled a little.

"I know it's not you," she said. "Sometimes I just stare into the future and don't like anything I see."

I knew her future as well as she knew mine. We would go where Kreon said, do what Kreon decreed. We lived by Kreon's mercy and we died by Kreon's might.

"Marrying Haemon won't be so bad," I said.

"What do you know?" she said. "You'll never fear your wife. But every wife fears her husband, even if she doesn't say so." She stuck her thumbnail between her teeth and bit down. A moment later, she added, "I don't give a shit about Haemon anyway. That's not what I mean."

"Well, if everything goes right tonight . . ."

She laughed at me.

I said, "You don't have faith in me?"

"It's not you I don't have faith in," she said, "it's 'things going right.'"

"Well, I need you to find some." I reached into the bag hanging off the back of the chair and took something out. It was a metal instrument about the size of my hand. Pointed at one end, thick at the other, almost like a syringe. An Extractor. I put it on the table between us.

She recoiled from it like it was a snake.

"Just in case," I said.

"Get that thing away from me. You're not dying."

"Just in case."

She leaned over the table, her wide eyes fixed on mine.

"Do you have any idea what it would do to me if I lost you?" she said in a harsh whisper.

"Yeah, I kinda do," I said. "Same as what it would do to me if I lost you. And lately that seems more and more likely."

"What's that supposed to mean?"

The thing about her was, nobody could hide from her, but she thought she could hide from everybody. Like she was some great actress. Like I wouldn't notice my own sister going limp by fractions, all the fight gone out of her.

"Sometimes you stare into the future," I said, "and you don't like anything you see."

"Don't you dare tell me you're doing this for me."

"Not just you. God, how long do you think we can go on this way? Any of us?"

A city of seven districts. Kids chanted about it in the North: *Seven houses crumbling on a Theban street. One's got no fire, one's got no heat. One's got no water; one's got no meat.* Saw them once jumping rope to it; got scattered a few minutes later by the police.

Antigone touched the Extractor with just her fingertips.

"What if I don't believe in this shit?" she said, nodding to the instrument. "What if I don't think a person can be reborn?"

"You don't?"

"I don't know."

"Well, doesn't really matter either way, does it?" I said. "I believe in it. And if I die, I want you to promise to store my ichor in the Archive. I want you to make sure I can be remade. Consider this my will and testament. Okay?"

"Okay," she whispered.

"Promise?"

"My word is my word," she said, scowling at me. "But yes, I promise. If you promise not to plan on dying."

I smiled. "Promise."

She closed her eyes as another wave of wind swept across us, dusting our coffees. Tears spilled down her cheeks, and she wiped them away with her scarf. By the time the air settled again, she looked unaffected. She sipped her coffee, dust and all.

"This coffee is shit," she said.

"Everybody's a critic," I replied, and chugged the rest of mine.

3

Antigone

The Archive stood in the middle of the city, where the land sloped steeply upward into a hill that looked more like a shelf. It was a building of chalky beige stone, and the land surrounding it was the same, rough and bare. It had been so difficult to move materials up there, the story went, that no one had wanted to repeat the experience, so the Archive was a lonely place, a place for pilgrims.

I worked my way down narrow side streets, where my fine clothing drew the eyes of those who wanted to sell or pilfer, and my recognizable face sent those eyes away almost in the same moment. Still, wherever I went there was the jingling of change in cups, voices strained by coughing up dust asking me to buy, church tracts pressed into my hands that I let fall rather than grasp. I should have had an escort. I was viable and young. Like a crystal glass, fragile and precious and useful only for what I might contain.

All the buildings in this part of the Electran District were worn by weather and wind, but covered in colorful graffiti, some more artful than others. I paused by a scene of a boat in the midst of a stormy sea, a cartoon duo boxing in a ring with gloves made of rock, a woman's face with a name and date scrawled beneath it. I walked past little shops with no signs: Hardware stores that were just rows of buckets with nails and bolts in them, electronics stores advertising access to the old Internet for ten spend a minute, bakeries stacked high with bread loaves behind bars.

I reached the steps at the foot of the hill, and waited in line to climb them. They were wide enough for one person going up and one person going down. My feet ached in flat sandals. I had not planned to come here. But with Polyneikes' "just in case" Extractor weighing down the bag at my side, I had no other choice.

On the steps, the man in front of me was counting every time he picked up his foot. I wondered who he was going to visit—a spouse gone before him, or a child gone too soon. Or maybe he was going to prepare a place for himself. It was possible even for the poor to find a place in the Archive now. My father's law, my father's doing. I listened to the feeble voice in front of me saying, "Thirty, thirty-one, thirty-two." *Immortality,* I had once heard my father say, *should be for everyone.*

The back of my neck was slick with sweat by the time we reached the top, the old man's counting now in the shape of a harsh exhale. The straps of my sandals had worn blisters into my heels and toes. There were people sitting on the rocks at the top, resting, staring out at the city—the dust-haze moved through the streets, the bumps of short buildings and the sheen of their windows and the rolling hills that surrounded us on all sides too distant to be clear. I could only see their faint ripple against the sky.

Beyond the hills was wilderness in every direction. I'd never been out there, but my father had told me it was exactly what I would expect: ruins.

From there I could see the High Commander's house to the east, in the Seventh District, a grand, sprawling structure with an open courtyard that was a market, an oddity, a place of public pronouncements and demonstrations. Not far from it was the Trireme, our beacon of hope.

The Trireme was a ship, but the ocean would never touch its hull. Instead it would leap into the stars that enfolded us—it would leap as high as it could go, and send out a signal that said, *we are here, help us,* to whoever might be listening. Our planet was a tomb, but hope still lived in the Trireme for the rock to be rolled away, for the grave to be unearthed.

It reflected the bright clouds back at me. I turned away and walked toward the Archive.

At the entrance, I removed my shoes with a sigh of relief and let them dangle from my fingertips by their straps. As I passed between the columns at the entrance, cool air washed over me and I sighed again.

It was dark—early superstition had said that too much light might compromise the samples, though we knew now that wasn't the case. But where there was light, it was warm, almost orange, thanks to the color of the high stone walls. Rows and rows of shelves confronted me, narrow, and I thought of the photographs I had seen of grand libraries from other eras, housing books instead of gametes. There were still books, of course, but time had devoured them. They existed digitally, but accessing them was onerous—you had to find a port, pay for your time, and download what you wanted to your own device, which was likely finicky and prone to malfunction.

I counted the fourth row from the left and walked down the aisle, a few paces behind two women who walked with hands clasped, whispering to each other. The one on the left wore her hair loose over her shoulders; she threw it back and leaned into the one on the right, smiling. The one on the right glanced back at me and released her partner's hand abruptly. It wasn't uncommon for two women to come here under the guise of friendship to make a child together. They would explore the Archive together, and then one of them would meet with an Archivist alongside a man willing to play the part. The Archivist, none the wiser, would help them narrow down the kind of resurrection they wanted to facilitate.

I turned at the end of the row to give them privacy. I knew what it was to be something you were not permitted to be.

My existence, as well as my siblings', was blasphemous. People didn't resurrect their own genes—to do so was considered dangerous, for practical as well as mystical reasons. We were each of us born with a virus, passed on from mother to child, and there was no cure. It deteriorated our genetic code from the moment we were born, introducing abnormalities, aberrations. Genes therefore needed to be edited before they were passed on, so that every child could be born with a clean slate—so that they wouldn't die young, as my siblings and I would.

But for the mystics, not the scientists, there was another crime in having a natural-born child. Each person's ichor was like a tapestry containing the many threads of those who lived before. When combined with another person's ichor, that tapestry grew richer and more complex. But ichor couldn't convey the soul through the cells until a person's death. Having a child of your own flesh, while you were still alive, meant having a child who wasn't a part of that tapestry. It meant having a child who had no soul.

Like me.

In the gap between the shelves, I saw the couple stop near the end of the row. The woman on the right tugged the placard out of its place next to one of the samples, and they both crouched to read it, the woman on the left resting her chin on the other's shoulder. I could have moved past them, but I lingered, watching them instead as they read the summary of a life they found on the little metal sheet.

They would choose two souls in the Archive that they found worthy of resurrection, and in doing so, at least in theory, they would choose their child's story before they were born. I wondered what kind of story these two would want. A quiet life, maybe, unremarkable but peaceful, kind. Or perhaps—drama, a tragic end, a life of tumult and potential. In the Archive, you could read a person's story and remake it. Combine it with another pattern, to heighten it or temper it. The possibilities were endless, overwhelming.

It didn't matter if a person wanted a child or not. It didn't matter if they changed the rest of their body, if they embraced a new name—if they were viable, the state considered them a woman, and they were required to carry a child, even though only half of them would survive it. Our species would die without this law, people were so fond of saying. And perhaps they were right about that. Every year, we were shrinking. Contracting. Receding.

Regardless, I didn't see, in the women who walked beside me, separated by shelves of samples, any hesitation, any resentment. That their bodies were considered vessels for the continuation of the species rather than things that belonged solely to them did not appear to weigh on them. They looked caught up in this mystical alchemy, genes and ritual stirred together in the incense- and dust-saturated air of the Archive.

Or maybe I was just seeing what I expected to see. Pol often said that I saw the world in extremes. And I often reminded him that it was an extreme world.

The couple turned at the next throughway, and I continued ahead to the sealed records at the very back of the space, where the famous, the notorious, the prominent were kept. Their genes couldn't be repurposed without express permission from the state. That was where my parents' ichor resided.

Ichor, I heard my mother say, sneering, in the back of my mind.

No one likes to use the technical terms for things, do they? Not enough romance in "egg" and "sperm" for them.

I was sure that Kreon would hold my parents' ichor hostage, using the threat of their permanent destruction to control us. We couldn't resurrect them, but as long as they were stored here, someone could. One day. And I had believed in resurrection, once. Even now that I didn't . . . Pol, Ismene, and Eteocles still did, and I wouldn't be the one to take the hope of my parents enduring away from them. And so the axe blade was always dangling over us.

It was even darker here, the channels cut in the ceiling farther apart. Each sample occupied a space the size of a book, making the library comparison even more apt. During the day, a dim light glowed beneath each one, to illuminate the name written on a label beneath. In a slot beside them was a slate with a description of their lives. I didn't need the label to find my father and mother, settled next to each other in a place of prominence, near the front. Oedipus. Jocasta.

Oedipus, who would have been our first freely elected leader. Jocasta, who sought to give childbearing to everyone—thus freeing those who didn't want it. A scientist in a city where only men were scientists; an impossibility of a woman.

Some people came to the Archive to grieve. I heard their whispers even then, like a distant stream. I wondered what they said to the dead. I didn't come here to tell my mother and father my secrets, my sorrows, and my regrets. I came here because it was the only place where Kreon wasn't watching. I knelt on the stone floor in front of my parents' names, set my sandals down, and opened my bag. I took out the Extractor and held it up to the light.

It was one of my mother's old ones, I was sure. We had so little of her, of him. Distributing their possessions was a rite of mourning, and we had not been permitted to mourn. The closest Ismene and I had come was preparing the bodies. I had stripped them bare; Ismene had washed them. Ismene had said the prayer; I had done the Extraction, plunging one instrument into my father's body, two inches below the belly button, and another into my mother's. It could only be done on the dead. I closed my eyes, and forced myself to imagine doing it to Polyneikes, but try as I might, I couldn't envision him dead. He was only ever sleeping.

I put the Extractor back in my bag, and took a deep breath. The name "Jocasta" was scribbled in poor handwriting on the label. It took me a few seconds to remember that it was mine. Those days had passed in a fog.

"Hello, dear," came a soft voice on my right.

I jerked to attention. Standing at the end of the short aisle was Eurydice, Kreon's wife.

People called her the angel of Thebes. She was fine boned and delicate. Her skin was so pale that in sunlight, you could see right through it to the blue veins and straight tendons beneath.

"Hello." I picked up my sandals and stood. There was dust on my knees, dust on my heels.

"I apologize for interrupting," she said. "I came here to see my own mother, and thought I would say hello to yours on my way out."

"Your mother is still here?" I asked. Though children weren't permitted to resurrect their parents—it was considered incestuous, as well as selfish, not to contribute to genetic diversity—a prominent family like hers was a desirable one, in the Archive. I had assumed that someone would have brought Eurydice's mother forth by now.

"My mother was a Follower of Lazarus," Eurydice said. "She'll be here until the end of everything. Or so she believed."

Followers of Lazarus—we called them "Fools," an easy nickname, hand delivered. They believed a creator would raise them from the dead via their ichor when the world ended, and as such,

they requested that their material be used only if there was no
alternative. It was noted on their placards in red. My mother had
criticized them regularly, claiming that looking forward to the
end meant no longer striving for survival, no longer valuing humanity. Despite that, I felt more kinship with them now than I
ever had. Sometimes the end was all there was left to long for.

"But you don't agree with her," I said.

Eurydice smiled. "No. I believe in the enduring nature of the
soul, as she did, but I don't believe in the end."

"I don't think I believe in either," I said, and in this place that
so many thought of as holy, it felt like a confession. I touched
my mother's name with just my fingertips. "I don't think if I used
her ichor I would get her back. I think she's gone."

"Those two things do not have to coincide," Eurydice said.
"If a soul endures, then perhaps—it simply endures, no matter
what we do. If not in ichor, then elsewhere."

"How do you know a soul even exists?" I said.

"I suppose I don't," Eurydice said. "I simply don't prioritize
certainty."

Her eyes were gentle. It was tempting to think of her as a
flimsy thing. But no flimsy thing could have been with Kreon for
so long and remained herself.

"Shall we go?" I said. "Or do you want a moment alone with
her?"

I nodded toward my mother's slot. Eurydice just shook her
head, and we walked together down the aisle. I thought of the
couple from earlier, finishing their perusal, talking about the kind
of child they wanted. Once they made their selections, down the
road, the Archivist would combine the cells they selected, the
souls they selected, and implant them in one of their wombs.
After that, I wasn't sure. Maybe she would die in childbirth. Sta-
tistically, it was as likely as survival. But even if she did survive—
women were protected by the home, and only men could move

freely outside of it. Would those women raise a child with two men who favored each other? Would they try to scrape together a life on their own? The memory of them scolded me. What a small creature I was to fear and hate the thing they were risking everything for. But a small creature I was, and I could not be otherwise.

The air was hot outside the Archive, and it was always strange to go places with Eurydice, who was the closest thing to royalty that existed in our city. People gathered around her like suppliants, eyes sparkling, mouths smiling, hands reaching. She was overwhelmed by them, searching for exits, but I couldn't help her. Their eyes skipped over me as if I wasn't there. It was kinder than acknowledging what I was.

Her eyes fixed on something in the distance, and the smile she gave was relieved. Kreon's face surfaced from the crowd and I fought all my instincts to recoil. He was surrounded by space, as if he emitted a repulsive force. He walked up to Eurydice, taller than she was and broader, and kissed her cheek. Everyone around us watched.

Lingering a few feet behind him was my eldest brother, Eteocles. Our eyes met.

"Brother," I said. "I trust you're here to visit our parents."

"Hello, Antigone," he said with obvious unease.

Eteocles was Kreon's shadow, these days. He hardly took a step without clearing it first.

"Antigone," Kreon said in what might have sounded like warmth if his eyes were not so full of scrutiny. He didn't bend toward me to kiss my cheek. He never touched any of us if he could help it, as if our profound emptiness could leech the life from his body if he did.

"Uncle," I replied.

"You're alone?" It was clear he didn't approve. "Did you come to pay your respects to the dead?"

"I came to ask a question," I said.

"Did you receive an answer?"

So many were listening to us. I smiled.

"I'm at peace," I said. "That's answer enough."

Kreon's eyes glittered as they met mine. Over his shoulder, Eteocles' eyes darted from mine to Kreon and back again.

"I am glad to hear it," Kreon said.

What came next was a script of courtesy. Kreon ensured that I would return home. Eurydice would remain a bit longer, waiting for him to finish his business, and Eteocles would accompany me back to the house. God forbid I be alone.

In silence I descended the steps behind the older of my two brothers. *One, two, three . . .*

4

Eurydice

My mother thought I was a prophet. I was never clear on why. She would just say she felt it in her bones, like that was enough. Only no child wants to be taken as seriously as my mother took me. Every word that fell out of my mouth had meaning, to her. So I stopped talking. I must have gotten used to it, because sometimes it was still hard for me to find the words.

My mother was always looking for something bigger, something more. She was always looking for an ending. Maybe that's why she chose one for herself when reality failed to satisfy. When the prophet daughter had nothing to say. Silence, I suppose, is its own kind of message and its own kind of ending. Just not one that anyone wants to hear.

I visited her every week without fail. I liked the walk to the Archive, even with Nikias a few paces behind me as a silent protector. I liked to stand at the top of the hill and look at the city and recall its size. So often it felt too fragile, like the very foundation of it was about to crumble. But nothing so big, so sprawling, could be so easily felled.

I hadn't expected to see Kreon here. He didn't make a habit of coming to the Archive, because walking among the dead wasn't useful, and he did like to be useful. He looked out at the Trireme, fixed in the launch position, and I looked at the corner of his jaw, rough with a beard.

"What brings you here?" I said to him. We were surrounded by guards, but that was always true. I felt like we were alone.

"Heli, who oversees the Seventh," he said. "His daughter is here. She got into some trouble, and he asked me to handle it myself, as a personal favor to him." He turned toward me and took my hands. "I'd like you to come with me. I'm sure your presence could only be helpful to her."

He wasn't asking, but I nodded. He moved my hand to the crease of his elbow, and together we walked alongside the Archive building to the back, where the laboratories were. As we walked, I looked up at the row of columns that framed the building, worn by the wind. I had lived forty years and still I marveled that something weak could wear away at something strong, given enough time. A raindrop tunneling through a mountain, a breeze smoothing the rough edges of stone.

"You shouldn't be seen so often with our niece in public," he said to me as we walked. "That's twice in two weeks now."

"It is seen as compassion," I replied.

"Today it is," he said. "Tomorrow they may remember too clearly what she is."

His lip curled, and I recalled the day his brother and sister-in-law were killed in the street, how he asked about the children with hope in his voice. He would never dishonor his family by striking out at them, but he had thought perhaps the violence of the riot had solved his problems for him. I had never tasted such rage as I felt that day.

The back of the Archive was smooth, faultless stone with no windows. I released Kreon's arm to let him precede me into the building. There, attendants sprang to their feet to greet him—and me—with respect. They offered us tea, and figs, and a place to sit, and Kreon refused all. He asked to see *the girl,* and one of the attendants rushed ahead to ready her.

"Remember to be soft," I said to him, as we waited. "If she is in trouble—"

"I will be what I am," he replied firmly. "For softness, I have you."

Had I always been soft? It was difficult to say. I was a willful child. The scars on my knuckles—the punishments of frustrated teachers—testified to that. So, too, my refusal to speak to my mother, knowing she would weigh every word that came from my lips too heavily. But I was soft with Kreon. I saw in him what others didn't.

The attendant gestured to us, and we followed her down a long, dim hallway to one of the examination rooms. This was a place for everything related to childbearing. Jocasta had once worked here, hidden in the back so none would see that the laboratory was occupied by a woman. I came with her once to look at her work, but I couldn't make sense of all the glass tubes, the worn books, the glowing microscope.

We stopped before the laboratories this time, and the attendant led us into an examination room. It was small, with an exam table and a stool and a small cabinet full of equipment. Lying atop the table, her body covered in a white sheet, was Clio, daughter of Heli, steward of the Seventh District.

She was hardly more than a child, her cheeks round, her body slender as a deer. Her eyes were unfocused and red with tears. A clump of hair clung to her lip, unnoticed. She saw Kreon, and she struggled to sit up.

"Please, be still," I said. "We come as friends."

Kreon raised an eyebrow at this, but didn't contradict me.

"Is my father angry with me?" she said, her voice small and scraped.

"Does he have reason to be?" Kreon said.

"I don't—" She choked a little, and looked away. We waited in silence for the end of the sentence, which didn't come.

I laid a hand on Kreon's shoulder.

"Let me speak with her," I said.

"Heli asked—"

"Heli asked you to handle this personally," I said. "And what am I but an extension of you?"

Kreon's eyes softened by a fraction. He nodded and stepped out of the room. I could feel something ease in the air after his departure, like a strong wind had settled.

I drew the stool to the side of the exam table, and perched on top of it. Clio's hands were folded over her abdomen, her nails bitten down to the quick. There was a poster on the wall beside her, a diagram of the woman's reproductive system. Poised above the pink of the uterus was a slim needle—an Extractor, to show the correct angle of approach.

"I came for a pregnancy test," Clio said. "The Archivist called my father."

"I see."

"At first, he thought—" She closed her eyes. Tears ran down her temples and into her hair. "He called me a wild girl."

"But you aren't," I said.

She shook her head.

"And now your father is at home sharpening his blade," I said. "And he wishes to know where to point it."

Clio's eyes were hazel, an in-between color. One moment they were blue, and the next, brown.

"Is it strange," she said, "that I am not eager for this man's death?"

I reached for her hand and she gave it to me, letting me lace my fingers with hers and squeeze.

"We punish few crimes as severely as this one," I said. "As

bearers of children, we are sacred vessels in need of protection."
It was a line directly from a pamphlet my mother gave me when
I was ten years old and started to bleed. I quoted it without
meaning to. It was so embedded in my mind, in my memory. "If
we didn't punish this crime with death, it might become more
common. And that would compromise the vigor of our society.
With each violation of that vigor, we become more fragile and
susceptible to loss. So this is not about revenge, Clio. It is about
stability. Do you understand?"

She squeezed my hand so tightly it caused pain. She squeezed
her eyes shut, too, her body braced against whatever came next.

"Eneas," she said, the name breaking from her like a scream.

I kept hold of her hand.

"Thank you," I said. "You've done everything you were supposed to. Okay?"

She nodded, and when I opened my hand, she opened hers.

"Do you want me to call your mother here?" I asked as I stood.

"My sister," she said. She was still tense, bent inward like a
hand cramping after too much writing. I had done that to her,
I knew. In the service of law and order, but not in the service
of her. Guilt rose up in me like bile from a sour stomach, and I
swallowed it down.

"I'll let them know," I said, and I turned toward the door. Just
before I opened it, her voice stopped me.

"I have to keep it. This . . . *soulless* thing," she said. "Don't I?"

I looked at my hand on the handle. Trembling.

"Every life is essential," I said quietly.

I left.

5

Ismene

"You can't stay for dinner?"

She wrapped her arms around my waist and pulled me back against her body. She was warm. My height, perfectly aligned. I felt her mouth against my shoulder, against my throat. I smiled, turning my face so she couldn't see it, and covered her hands with my own.

She was a singer. I heard her once while walking through the market, in the evening when I was long past my unstated curfew. The sun had set, but there was still some light in the sky, and as I moved through the crowd a rich alto reached my ears. I followed the sound to her—she was picking through an array of scarves at a woman's clothing stall, her fingers long and elegant. When she caught me staring, she raised an eyebrow. *What? You have something to say, rich girl?* When I stammered through an apology, she only laughed.

She hummed now, and I felt the vibration of it against my back.

"I can't stay," I said. "I have to go back."

"Is someone counting down the minutes?"

I couldn't explain it to her. That would require admitting who I was, which inevitably led back to *what* I was: a jug without water to fill it, a shell without a nut, a lantern with no flame. I had given her a name that wasn't mine, a name that wasn't anyone's. It was easier than risking her disgust.

Below, the street was crowded with food stalls. The smell of smoke and cooked corn and fried bread wafted up through the curtains.

Instead of answering, I turned in her arms and ran my fingers along her collarbone. Her skin was sticky with sweat. I touched my lips to hers.

"I have to go," I said again, and she sighed.

I slipped on my sandals and left. Once on the street below, I didn't look back to see if she was watching me go. Our time was at an end. I wouldn't see her again. That was what happened when I started to feel like there was a string connecting me to another at the sternum, when my refusals were no longer sufficient for either of us.

It wasn't built to last anyway. My path was set.

I tugged the bars out of place on the cellar window and stuck my feet in. With a glance down the alley to the left and to the right to make sure no one was watching, I shimmied through the small opening and dropped down on flat feet into the storage room, between two sacks of grain. I stood on my tiptoes to put the bars back in place, and then picked up an empty bottle from one of the shelves near the door, as if I had merely come here for a new water jug. It was a plausible enough explanation. Household staff didn't like to talk to us if they could avoid it, so they didn't ask many questions.

I made it all the way back to our wing of the house before

I saw anyone. Eti stood at my door, his fist raised to knock, a flower in his hand. He smiled at me in greeting, but the smile faded too quickly.

"Where were you?" he said. "You look flushed."

I held up the empty bottle. "I broke mine. Decided to fetch myself another."

"That's the second bottle you've broken in a week," he said. "Who is she?"

I took the flower from him and opened my door with my shoulder. "Did you clip this from Kreon's greenhouse?"

It was just the end of a stem, but it had a few blooms on it, big draping purple things. I put it in the glass of water on my bedside table and carried it to the window. That way the sun would shine through the petals in the morning.

"It's monkshood," he said. "So don't eat it. It's poison."

"Is that its only purpose?" I said. All flowers had to have purpose, now, or they wouldn't be taking up space in a greenhouse.

"Yes," he said. "I believe so."

"What a shame," I said. "It's so pretty. Thank you."

"You didn't answer my question."

"She's no one," I said. "It was nothing. You don't need to worry."

"Others are allowed to have nothings. Not us."

I didn't correct him, but he was wrong. *He* was allowed certain liberties: stolen moments with a lover, an older woman who could no longer bear, anyone who was outside of a man's protection. But until I was married, I was Kreon's to guard, and not to be touched. If I didn't let myself have nothings, I would have nothing.

"Eti," I said. "Let it go."

"All right," he said. "I'm sorry."

I still felt her arms around my waist. I watched my brother

go, and in his absence, I could believe that I really was empty, as the mystics said.

Later that night, all I could see was the flower's outline against the window. The moon was bright as daylight. I kept fading in and out of sleep and thinking about why Kreon kept poison in the greenhouse next to the potatoes and the wheat. I wiped my palms on my pillowcase and got up to move the flower away from the windowsill. A breeze wafted in, pressing my nightgown tight to my body. Then I heard a knock.

It was Antigone's knock, four sharp taps. I pulled the stopper from beneath the door—wedged there to keep unwanted people out as I slept—and opened to my sister's worried eyes. She wore her robe cinched tightly around her waist and sandals on her feet.

"Can I come in?" she said.

I stepped back to let her in, then looked down the hallway in both directions to make sure no one was watching. The hallway was quiet and still, but even that was no guarantee. There was always someone following Antigone in this house. But there was nothing too interesting about sisters seeking comfort with each other.

"Are you all right?" I said to her. She paced toward the middle of my room, where a worn rug covered the stone floor, and then back to me. She was picking at her fingernails like she was plucking guitar strings.

"I have a bad feeling," she said.

Antigone had bad feelings about everything lately. Her life seemed to be weighed down by dread. Dread of Haemon, dread of a child—as if the more attachments she formed, the more she would wither away. But that wasn't how it had to work. I had as many obligations as she, and half her misery.

"A bad feeling about what?"

She looked away.

"There's just something in the air," she said.

She was never a good actress.

"You know something you don't want me to know," I said.

Pacing again. "I don't *know* anything. That's the problem."

Sighing, I caught her by the wrist and led her toward the bed.

"You can't predict the future," I said. "You can't feel bad things coming, and you can't make them come by feeling them."

She nodded. She still looked frantic, and her color was off, but she sat on the edge of the mattress.

"Come on, let's have a sleepover," I said. "It'll be easier to sleep that way."

She frowned at me. Maybe she was remembering all the sleepovers we had as girls. We would pull the mattress off the bed—Father scolded us for this, since the floor was dirtier than the bed frame—and gather as many pillows as we could from the rest of the house, including the couch cushions, and hang a sheet over the whole nest of down so it felt like we were inside a cloud. Then we would try to stay up all night. Antigone never made it, but I did. I had no shortage of memories to keep me awake, even when both our parents were alive and we knew nothing about the world's troubles yet.

Antigone liked to say we had been doomed from the start. We came from excess—our parents' hedonistic desire to see themselves replicated without refinement, heedless of our souls. As a result, I carried too many of yesterday's woes. Antigone carried too many of tomorrow's. And Polyneikes carried too many of today's.

Eteocles, well . . . Eti was a hard person to know.

This sleepover felt different than the ones in our youth. Heavy with dread. Antigone and I lay on top of the blankets, shoulder to shoulder, sharing the corners of the same pillow. I closed my eyes and tried to find something settled inside myself. But the monkshood was still on the desk, lush and purple, and the hum of anxiety was running down Antigone's arm like an electric current. Her fingers hooked around mine. Her hands were tacky with sweat. So were mine.

We didn't speak. There was nothing to say.

I dropped off at some point—from sheer boredom, probably—and woke to a clatter.

Antigone was already at the edge of the bed, her hair loose around her shoulders and wild, her feet shoving into sandals. Before I could even say her name, she was throwing my door open and racing down the hallway, and I had no choice but to follow. I ran barefoot down the hall, the stone scraping my heels, and chased her down the stairs and around the bend to the courtyard. I heard distant screams. None of the guards were where they were supposed to be. Everything felt empty and strange, like the world had ended and we had slept through it.

We tumbled into the courtyard together, where ivy grew like fungus on the walls, and the stones were rougher, paler. They cut my feet. The doors to the street were wide open, the bar that usually held them closed lying in the dust. Men were tangled together in the courtyard itself, and everywhere was grunting and groaning and the sound of metal hitting metal. Screams of pain, screams of names, screams of last words intended to fill the night but instead fading into the din. And in the center of the courtyard, two bodies.

My mother once told me she knew me from a distance because of the way I walked. *How do I walk?* I asked her, full of adolescent insecurity. She only shrugged. *Like my daughter,* she replied.

It was in that way that I recognized the bodies in the middle of the courtyard as my brothers.

Antigone sprinted right into the middle of the fray, ducking under a swinging arm. She fell to her knees beside one of the bodies. The fight was already ending. There was no surrendering. No raised palms, no swords laid down, nothing but fleeing or dying.

"Get her away from him!"

Kreon's voice rang out from one of the balconies. He stood there, his chest bare and scarred from his years in the military police, his shorn head reflecting moonlight. He extended a long arm and pointed at Antigone, who was sobbing over our brother's body; I couldn't tell which one, Polyneikes or Eteocles, though I knew they were both dead.

One of the guards grabbed her by the shoulders and lifted her like she was nothing. She squirmed and kicked, but she was small—smaller than me, even—and there was nothing she could do. The guard dragged her away flailing and undignified.

I stood under the fall of ivy. There were bodies all over the courtyard. Their blood looked black. I stepped over one, careful, and then another. My footprints left wet impressions on the stone. A guard held out an arm to stop me from going any closer to my brothers. I stopped just behind it, obedient.

My brothers wore identical wounds, just under their ribs. Clutched in their fists—Eteocles' right and Polyneikes' left—were identical weapons, short pistols from Kreon's stores. Eteocles', given to him by Kreon, a reward for his loyalty. Polyneikes', likely stolen. There was no one near them. It seemed clear to me, based on how each of them had fallen, that they had fired at each other, one in opposition to our uncle and one in defense of him.

Doomed from the start, I found myself thinking. *All of us.*

6

Antigone

We didn't have many pictures of us as children, but in the few we did have, I was indistinguishable from Polyneikes. Both born with a thick head of dark hair, a ready smile, a dimple in one cheek but not the other. He kept the smile. I kept the dimple. We called them "our" baby pictures because it was never certain who was who.

We were a rarity among rarities: twins, in a world where siblings weren't even genetically related, where the living only ever came from the scrubbed, polished dead. We were made of the same substance, two parts of one whole, the most abominable of abominations. *One age's horror is another age's wonder,* my mother said once, mildly, as she poured herself a drink. It was as much of a defense as she had ever offered for her choice.

Two parts of one whole, and I felt the loss of him that way, as the loss of a leg, an arm, a lung, a kidney.

They locked me in my room, but they needn't have bothered. I sat on the edge of my bed, one sandal on and the other lost by the doorway as I kicked and scratched at the guard dragging me away from my brother's body.

I watched the sun come up.

A knock came, and for a single, beautiful moment I thought it was him, come to tell me it had all been a ruse, a trick, and the revolution had succeeded because of it, and that was why he hadn't been able to tell me, because the whole operation hinged on no one knowing, and he was sorry, so sorry to have put me through all that, but we were free now—

Right. The knock.

Kreon's son, Haemon, walked into my room with the air of someone who knew he was somewhere he shouldn't be. We were betrothed, but the arrangement didn't include any intimacy. It had been Kreon's idea, a way of consolidating power. The daughter of his greatest challenger conceding to his rule by marrying his son. An act of mercy, some said, toward a broken, cursed girl. An act of foolishness, others said, to marry one's only son to someone who might not have a soul.

Haemon was tall and broad, his skin sun-warmed and his face carved from stone. He looked like he had been designed specifically for Kreon to love him, and perhaps that was exactly what had happened—maybe Haemon's entire being had been Eurydice accepting her husband's limitations, as she always did, and easing his way for him.

He stood like a soldier. His face betrayed no sympathy for me.

I was glad. I could not have withstood it.

"Hello," he said, and it was like an apology.

I cleared my throat.

"I assume you're here with a message from your father," I said.

"No," he said. "May I sit?"

I gestured to my desk chair. The wicker strained under his weight when he sat. He looked too big for it.

"I woke to chaos," he said. "But I wanted to see if you were . . ."

He trailed off.

"I suppose that makes sense," I said. "After a destructive event, what's the first thing people do? Survey the damage."

"Antigone, that's not—"

"Well, I'm damaged. You've seen. You can go now."

"I wanted to see if you were *all right*," he said, scowling at me.

"You knew I wasn't all right."

He sagged a little, like a clothesline weighed down by too many sheets, like a tree after a downpour. He stood and faced the window, his hands clasped at the small of his back.

"Yes, I did," he said.

"You came to tell me something," I said. "Better get on with it."

I tried to see the courtyard below through his eyes. The vines clinging to the edge of the window. The dry roots of the cypress below, bulging from the earth.

What did he love? What did he know?

"My father," he said slowly, "has decreed that your brother's body is not to be touched. It will be used as a warning against insurrection."

"Not to be touched," I said.

"Not to be *Extracted*," he said. "Excluded from the Archive."

The words were like cold water spilling down my spine.

"What?"

Haemon looked at me. Then looked away.

"That was his decree earlier this morning," he said. "Violators will be subject to the highest penalty."

"The *highest* penalty."

He gave me a pointed look.

"Execution," I said.

He nodded.

"Because Kreon thinks Polyneikes doesn't have a soul?" I demanded. "Or because of his crime?"

"I assume," Haemon said, "it's a combination of both. But the stated reason is the latter."

"Even my father was not excluded from the Archive," I said. "None of those who participated in the riots were, either."

"I know. Apparently he feels that a stronger tactic is needed to discourage further . . . attempts."

I knew there was nothing of Kreon in Haemon. He hadn't even provided the vessel in which Haemon grew to term. Still I wanted to hit Haemon and see if his father could feel it; I wanted to lash out as wild as I had been a few hours ago, struggling to get back to my brother.

Instead, I sat on the edge of the bed again. I dug the toes of my bare foot into the stone until it hurt.

"I'll leave you to your grief," he said.

The Extractor Polyneikes gave me was still in my bag, shoved under my bed with the spiders. I had not been able to imagine using it, not really, but now the absence of its weight in my hand felt like another thing excised from me. The most zealous in our city would say there was no point in storing Polyneikes' ichor because it was only cells, with no substance. But I knew my brother had a soul. I knew he was not empty.

Haemon paused by the door.

"I'll talk to him," he said, and my sharp laugh followed him out.

7

Ismene

One of the servants walked me back to my room, and I tried not to be offended that they didn't even think me troublesome enough to warrant a guard. She didn't speak to me, though I was desperate to hear something normal, some chatter about breakfast or discussion of the weather, something, anything to make the world feel like it had before, even if it was just for a second.

I went straight to the bathroom and stood in the tub as it filled, the water turning pink from the blood on the soles of my feet. Staring down at my toes, I got the unsettling feeling that I had been here before, and I remembered the art project we did in school, the teacher painting our palms and our feet and instructing us to make shapes on a big piece of paper with our footprints and handprints. We each got a color, and mine was red.

I looked again at the pale pink water, and vomited.

I moved through the rest of the morning like something was chasing me, urging me to move faster. Emptied the tub and scrubbed my legs and feet until they were flushed with color. Braided my hair and chose a dress. Chose a different one when

I remembered I was mourning. Laced my shoes tight around my ankles. Ate my breakfast in bits and pieces. Pinches of toast and bites of apple. Dry and sour and nauseating.

I heard the decree from there. Not the exact words, but the shapes of them, the timbre of Kreon's voice recognizable even through the windowpanes and walls. There were horns throughout our district for announcements such as these. I had stood beneath them before, to hear warnings for storms, for fire, for high levels of radiation, for curfews.

It was the maid who brought my lunch who told me what he said.

Then Eurydice came, with all the quiet that usually attended her, her eyes red and the fine hair that framed her cheeks a little wet, as if she'd splashed water on her face.

"I'm so sorry," she said.

I was crying. It had been happening all day, tears just leaking out of my body, as passive as bleeding.

"What for?" I asked her, a touch of bitterness in my voice. "Have you done something I'm not aware of?" I tilted my head. "Or perhaps failed to do something?"

She pressed her mouth into a line.

"I came to ask you if you'd like to perform Eteocles' Extraction," she said.

I felt as if I'd drunk poison. Bitterness filled my mouth, my throat. Bitterness soured my stomach and dried up my tears. To offer this to me as if it was a mercy was the height of cruelty. Of course I would perform Eteocles' Extraction. Of course Kreon would permit it—my brother had died defending him. Of course.

And Polyneikes would rot.

I followed her through the hallways to the courtyard. It was bright outside, the sky a white haze, and the rest of the bodies had been cleared from the courtyard. The bloodstains had been sprayed down and then covered with a fresh layer of dirt. The trampled plants had been removed by the root, the places they occupied packed down and smoothed over. And lying on his back under the cypress tree was Eteocles.

His skin was coated in dust. Blood had dried around his mouth. Someone had put his hands at his sides and straightened his legs, a posture he had never taken when alive, so he looked unlike himself—like a statue of my brother instead of the actual form of him. I stood at his feet for a few long moments.

Eteocles knew me, and I knew him. How he struggled to make sense of things, sometimes; how he found it easier to simply follow the rules. How he craved not praise but affirmation that he was doing what was expected of him. How he envied the lively energy of our twin siblings, and shared with me a desire to be like them, all edges, always on the verge of some kind of revelation. But we were not like them. We were like each other. Quiet and level. A cup of flour skimmed with the flat of a knife. A picture frame hanging just so on a wall. The click of a metronome.

Three elderwomen stepped out of the house. There were always three, waiting for the Extraction to be done. They would wrap the body in cloth and then carry it, two at the head and one at the feet. I looked over their rounded shoulders to the street beyond the courtyard, where a cart waited for Eteocles' body. They would take it back to the mortuary, and burn it.

There would be only women there. No man would dare touch a body, fearing its emptiness. Empty things were hungry. They wanted to take. But women were different. Once we could no longer bear life, our sole responsibility was to attend the dead.

"Can I have some water," I said to one of them. "And a cloth."

I knelt at his head and waited. The oldest of them—or so it seemed, her face had the deepest lines—brought me a small bowl of water with a folded scrap of linen a few minutes later, and I began to clean his face. I scrubbed at the dried blood around his mouth. I ran the wet cloth along his cheeks and brow. I discovered my father anew in his crooked nose, my mother in his attached earlobes.

When I was finished, Eurydice handed me an Extractor. I lifted Eteocles' shirt. There was a scar on his abdomen from an appendix removal. I touched four fingers to his cold stomach, below his belly button.

I was a woman, so this was my task, mine and Antigone's. We had learned the right procedures from our mother, and she had learned them from hers. No one had asked us if we wanted to. No one had asked us if we could bear it.

As it happened, I couldn't bear it, but I did it anyway.

I said the prayer. I plunged the Extractor in.

8

Antigone

Rumor—passed along by the maid who came to change my sheets later that morning—said that Polyneikes' body was on display in the street just north of Kreon's house, guarded by soldiers. As of twenty-four hours after his death, his ichor would no longer be viable, and the body would be removed.

They unlocked my door and I walked to the north end of the house, where two walls separated me from my brother's body. I thought about looking out the window to see the grotesque display, and my stomach roiled at the thought. When I left a few minutes later, I left through the back door and took the circuitous route, walking through the Neïstan District to get to the North District. When I turned back to see if I was being followed, I could just barely see the glimmer of the Trireme, nose pointed at the sky.

I expected my head to be busy, maybe even frantic. Instead, I felt stillness. I saw the sagging buildings, the shops with their beat-up pots and pans stacked high on the street, the food carts with smoke hanging around them like a cloud, the children selling bouquets of weeds, the drunk men slumped in doorframes, the old women sitting on front steps to stitch old garments, and I didn't think about my brother, about the Extractor in my bag, about his body as a crude monument to Kreon's cruelty. I didn't think about anything. I walked for the better part of an hour. The North District was the next one over from the Seventh, where I lived, but it was one of the larger ones; it spanned quite a few miles.

When I arrived at Parth's door, he greeted me with a nod and let me in. His apartment was on the ground floor, so all the noise of the street filled it. He lived there with several others whose names I didn't know and his mother, a wry, hunched woman with a scarf wrapped around her hair, who looked at me when I came in and said, "If I wasn't already dying, that face would probably kill me, girl."

"Don't look at it, then," I replied, and her laugh was like a wheeze.

Parth sat me down in his kitchen with a glass of water, and I waited for Ismene to arrive. I knew she would come, because I had asked her to, and Ismene always did what I asked her to. I was hoping that quality would extend beyond a long walk to the North District.

In the apartment above, someone was playing music. The bass rippled through the water in my glass, which sat untouched on the table. Some time passed before I heard Ismene's knock, a faint tap. She came into the kitchen, her hands folded in front of her. Her eyes were red with tears.

"Tig, what's this about?" she said, and I felt a deep ache. That name. Pol was the one who gave it to me, when we were children.

"Sorry," she said. "I didn't mean to—"

"I know," I said. "I just needed to talk to you someplace where I knew no one would be listening."

We both looked at the door separating the kitchen from the living room.

"Where I knew Kreon wouldn't be listening," I amended.

Ismene sat in the chair across from mine. I slid my water glass toward her, and she sipped from it as I reached into the bag at my side and took out the Extractor.

I set it on the table between us.

"That's one of Mom's," she said. Sharp-eyed as ever. She brushed it with her fingertips, reverent. "Where did you get it?"

"Polyneikes gave it to me yesterday," I said. " 'Just in case,' he said."

She tugged her hand back like the Extractor had bitten her. "You *knew*?"

"I didn't know anything," I said. "He wouldn't tell me anything."

"Oh, sure. Our brother was worried he might die," she said. "But why tell me? It's not like he's my brother, too, right?"

"I'm—"

"You're not sorry," she snapped. "The two of you have always been like this. As if swimming around in the same womb with him gave you a greater capacity to love him."

I didn't argue with her; there was no point. But the mystics believed that sharing a body with someone created a sacred connection, the bond of mother and child, the bond of husband and wife. Was it so difficult to believe, then, that sharing a body with my brother had forged a similar connection? As children, when he fell down, I cried. When he was ill, I vomited. What was I to do now that he was dead?

She dabbed at her eyes with her sleeve.

"It doesn't matter, now," she said. "None of it. Kreon's decree—"

"*Fuck* Kreon's decree," I said.

"You can't possibly think . . ." She scowled at me. "You're go-ing to do it anyway?"

"We don't exclude people from the Archive," I said. "We don't exclude murderers, or thieves, or rioters. We don't deny anyone their chance at immortality."

"They don't believe we have *souls,* Antigone."

"I don't care. I do."

"You don't even believe in immortality."

"He did."

"You obviously haven't been down to the street," she said. "Because if you had, you'd know there's nothing but space and guards around his body. There's no way you can even get near it."

"Not alone," I said. "But if I have help . . ."

"Help," she repeated. "From me?"

"Well I'm not going to ask Parth, known rabble-rouser," I said. "We're women. No one will think of us as a threat. No one will think of us at all."

"Until they watch us walk across the square to his body and arrest us!"

"We'll make a plan."

"A plan to become invisible?"

"Is it not worth the risk to you?" I said. "Not worth the *at-tempt?*"

"He killed our brother," she said.

"He *is* our brother," I said. "And he was the better man."

"You insult the one in an attempt to salvage the other?"

"Yes!" I said. "I'll do whatever I have to, to salvage him!"

Silence fell in the room next to ours, as Parth and his mother undoubtedly heard me. Ismene shook her head.

"You're suicidal."

"No. I'm just not a coward."

I regretted saying it a moment later, when she just stared at me with wide eyes, like she couldn't believe I could think so badly of her.

"It's not cowardice to run from an inferno rather than spit water at it," she said. "It's survival."

"What good is survival if you trade yourself away in the process?"

She got to her feet and smoothed her shirt, and I knew she was ready to leave.

"Don't make me hate you, Ismene," I said. "Not when I love you so much."

She didn't look back.

9

Antigone

When the four orphaned progeny of Oedipus and Jocasta—then adults, or nearly so—came to live in Kreon's house, we took only what we could carry, and we went on foot through a silent city still under military lockdown. Eyes peered at us through darkened windows as we passed, escorted by guards, and every so often, we heard taps as our father's sympathizers drummed their fingers on the glass. In one quarter, we paused to listen to the patter all around us, like rain blowing against a windowpane.

We walked a long way, as my mother had insisted on living close to the university, which was in the Proetid District, on the far side of the hill where the Archive stood. As we went, I thought about making a run for it. Fleeing the city. Taking my chances in the emptiness beyond it. But there was only death out there; my father had seen it. Every so often the university tried to make contact with anyone else, anywhere on the planet. But there was nothing. No signs of life. There was nowhere to run.

So I kept walking.

Eurydice greeted us at the courtyard entrance, which opened to the street, her warm smile at odds with the soldiers around us, there "for our safety," as Kreon had put it. What had been strange to me then was not the silence of our city or the guards prowling the streets to make sure everyone stayed inside or the phalanx of soldiers around us, but the game of pretend that everyone seemed to have agreed to without consulting me. Kreon making a show of his generosity, of his responsibility to his family. Eurydice giving us a tour of the house, unleashing us on the east wing to choose our bedrooms like it was a treat. Smile fixed, eyes sparkling.

Only their son, Haemon, had refused to play, his wary eyes meeting mine across the dinner table, his voice echoing through the hallways as he asked his father why there were so many guards stationed in the east wing. He treated us like the hostages we were, and in the weeks that followed our arrival, I found myself grateful for it. At least he was not lying to me.

But Polyneikes had been the reason we all learned to survive there. He learned our guards' names, developed private jokes with them. Cajoled Eurydice into giving us comforts—a little plant for Ismene's windowsill, a cup of tea for him every Sunday, a schematic drawing of the Trireme for my wall, and for Eteocles, a position assisting Kreon.

Looking back now, I wondered how early Polyneikes had become a revolutionary. It might have been upon our arrival. Perhaps he had intended Eteocles to become an informant. Perhaps he had thought it was a given that Eteocles would want to help him, just as I had thought it was a given that Ismene would want to help me.

How well, I wondered now, did I really know any of them?

After my confrontation with Ismene in Parth's kitchen, I took the long way back to the house, my hair bound up in a scarf so I was less likely to be recognized. I slipped into the house through the back entrance, walking through the kitchen, busy with dinner preparations, to the unadorned hallways where the household staff worked. I passed through the little courtyard on my way to the east wing, and Haemon was there, standing beneath the ivy.

After our betrothal was announced, I had heard some of the household staff discussing it—how little I deserved him, how any woman in the city would love to trade places with me. How could Kreon promise his son to such a warped creature? Who knew what her imperfect body, swimming with unedited genes, would do to a child?

But Kreon knew what I knew: that if he did not bind one of us to Haemon, we—or our children—would forever be Haemon's competition. And Kreon believed in eliminating the competition.

So Haemon and I were assigned to each other, and he became my adversary, the man I had not chosen, who I did not want and who did not want me. Yet standing there beneath the ivy, a look of concern on his face, his shirt pulling tight across his shoulders, I remembered that most people would have felt lucky to marry such a man. It was a shame, I thought, that they couldn't.

"Are you waiting for me?" I said.

"You left," he said. "I suppose I was . . . concerned."

"I needed some air," I replied. "I was in no danger."

"It's customary to take an escort."

"I like to walk alone."

"Hmm." Haemon set his jaw. "So you and your sister independently decided to walk alone at the same time?"

I tilted my head and studied him for a moment.

"Did your father send you to question me?"

"I am not nearly as much his errand boy as you suppose."

"I'm not sure you have any idea what I suppose about you."

"I know you think of me with dread," he said, and his eyes were sharp enough to cut me to the bone. "And I know you have no reason to. I do not keep hostages."

"No, perhaps you don't," I said quietly. "But you don't release them, either, do you?"

"If you'd like me to escort you out of the city and into the wilderness," he said, "I will. But I don't think that's where you want to be."

We had been told that this city was founded here because of its comparatively low radiation levels—that when our ancestors all had fled their homes, they had been armed with nothing more than a Geiger counter, and most of them had died on the journey. I might not have believed this, if my father had not been outside the city. Every politician was required to go out there at least once, to see firsthand what it was like. My father wasn't afraid, so he had gone often. He had shown me his hazmat suit once, and the device he had used to measure radiation levels—someone checked them every year, to see if they were decreasing, if there was a chance the planet was healing itself.

Eventually, it will, he had told me. *The only question is, can we survive long enough to see it?*

And that was the whole point of it all—the Archive, the gene editing, the compulsory reproduction, and even Kreon's obsession with stability. We just had to hang on until the rest of the planet was habitable again. The Trireme, gleaming in the middle of the city like a fallen star, was meant only as a desperate backup plan: send a signal begging for help, see if anyone answers. And it was not the one that most people put their faith in.

"No," I said. "Funnily enough, I would rather my insides not be devoured by radiation."

A hint of a smile passed over Haemon's lips.

"We are all hostages here," he said. "Held at knifepoint by our own planet. But we can make the best of what we're given, you and I. And I don't intend to cause you any more misery than you've already endured."

Haemon had never lied to me, had he?

But there was always a first time. One day soon, he would have more power over me than anyone. And it took a singular man not to misuse power. How singular was Haemon?

"Prove it," I said suddenly.

"What?"

"Prove it," I said again, and I stepped closer to him. "Help me."

He frowned. I reached into my bag, and took out the Extractor, just enough for him to see what it was.

"Help me," I repeated.

I watched him calculate. He looked up at the hazy sky.

"Okay," he said.

"Okay?"

"Yes," he said. "Meet me here at midnight."

"That's cutting it close," I said. Pol had died just after one in the morning. We only had until one o'clock tonight to perform the Extraction.

"It'll be enough. I need to prepare something first."

All I could do, for a moment, was blink.

Then I nodded.

The Extractor was a marvel. Most people regarded it as they would have a magic wand or a cursed amulet—as if it wasn't to be touched carelessly, as if they needed to pray to it, *worship* it, to make it do its work. Even my mother, so determined that we should know the proper names for things, hadn't been able to simplify its processes enough for me to understand. I relied on figurative language instead.

In the low belly was where it needed to go. I had practiced on Ismene once, when we were small. Laid all four of my fingers beneath her belly button to mark the place, and then jabbed her with a stick, harder than I meant to, so she had leapt up and slapped me in retaliation. When she had lain back down, I'd wriggled my fingers in the air over her pelvis, to signify the microscopic bugs that wriggled through her body in search of her ovaries. My teacher had called them that, reminded us that a mosquito could smell carbon dioxide from thirty feet away, so was it really so strange that the Extractor could seek out the right cells?

After it found them, it wrenched the ichor from the body, leaving destruction in its wake. An Extractor was too brutal in its work to be used on the living. It left bruises on the surface, and greater damage within.

After making my bargain with Haemon in the courtyard, I lay down on the bed with the Extractor in my left hand and felt beneath my belly button with my right for the place. I positioned the point of the device against my skin. This was how it would look to Polyneikes if he was still there, his soul trapped in his body, living on in his cells.

I prayed for cloud cover, because a darker night meant concealment, but the sky cleared while I ate dinner at my desk, and by the time midnight came the moon was bright enough to read by. Still, I dressed in my darkest clothes and tucked the Extractor into the waistband of my trousers, covered by a jacket to disguise its bulk. Satisfied by the quiet press of my feet on the stone, I walked to the fall of ivy where Haemon was waiting.

"Bright out," he said in greeting. "Not good for us."

"I'm cursed, haven't you heard?"

Haemon smiled, wry. "I don't believe in curses."

"Good for you," I said. "So what's the plan here?"

He shrugged. "I arranged a distraction earlier."

"You *arranged* it . . . how?"

"Just trust me. Let's go."

We walked across the courtyard and down the hallway to the kitchen, where a few of the staff were sitting, playing cards, a pile of dried corn kernels in the middle of the table serving as chips. Haemon's hand slid into mine, and my shock was the only thing that kept me from pulling away.

"Sorry to interrupt," he said. "Just sneaking out the back."

I tried for a smile, but it didn't feel right. He tugged me toward the door and I tripped after him, into the alley behind the house. It smelled like rot there, and broken glass crunched under my shoe soles.

His hand slipped away.

"Can't believe I forgot about poker night," he said.

"Poker night?"

"Every week they get together and play—I've joined them a few times."

It didn't fit in with my image of him, sitting at that grubby table in the kitchen where the cooks sat to peel potatoes after a long day, his elbows propped, sleeves rolled up, cards in hand. Even now he was too stiff for that, his shoulders pulled back in an imitation of a soldier's posture.

"You any good?"

He laughed. "No. Lost all my corn, every time. But as you can see, it helps to make the right people like you."

We reached the end of the alley and started down the street that led around the wide house. Ahead of us, obscured now by buildings, was the street where my brother's body was displayed. The moon glinted on half a dozen windows. The Extractor dug into my hip with each step.

The road bent around a corner of Kreon's house where the plaster had broken, showing the stone underneath. The foundation here was cracked, the building weathered by time even though it was the finest one in the city. Not even Kreon could escape deterioration. It was hard to imagine a time when it hadn't been this way—when plants grew untended in the wild, maintained by their own seeds spreading; when the plains beyond the city were overrun with animals that we had not bred ourselves; when genes persisted through the generations, presenting a person with their grandmother's brow, their great-grandfather's jaw. Everything required effort now. Everything required editing.

The street opened up in front of us. I saw the contours of the soldiers guarding it—not spread out as they likely were during the day, each one taking a corner, but gathered together around a small flame, lighting their cigarettes. Several yards behind them, a dark lump on the ground, was Polyneikes.

"Wait here," Haemon said to me. "Until they're distracted."

"How will I know?"

"It won't be subtle."

I stood in the middle of the street, in the dark, and waited. Haemon put his hands in his pockets and strolled toward the guards. They startled when they recognized him, like they had been caught in an indiscretion by Kreon himself. Haemon only waved a hand, dismissive.

"Got a spare?" he said to them.

One of them produced a fresh cigarette, and another held out his own so Haemon could light it. I saw a curtain shift in the building across the way, and then, somewhere down the block, there was a huge, resonant *boom*. The ground rumbled. A plume of fire stretched up from the street, followed by a cloud of smoke. Screams echoed through the city. Haemon looked at the guards with alarm.

"What the fuck—" one of the guards said.

"Well, what are you waiting for?" Haemon said. "Go!"

"But—" another said, gesturing behind him to Polyneikes' shape on the ground.

"I'm fully capable of watching a dead body," Haemon said. "Go!"

I started toward the square, cautious at first, and then as the guards took off in the direction of the explosion, I burst into a

run. I tripped into the square and fell to my knees next to Polyneikes' body.

Time slowed as I looked at him. I heard my heartbeat, the twin
thuds distinct, valves closing, valves opening.

Thump, thump.

He still looked like himself, but his body was covered in a
layer of pale dust. His arms rested at an awkward angle across
his torso, as if he had been dragged out here and then dropped
without ceremony. His shoes were gone. His shirt was soaked
with blood.

Thump, thump.

I reached for him, unable to stop myself. His wrist felt wrong,
too cold and too stiff. I choked on a sob as I lowered his arm,
tucking it close to his side. His skin was discolored, from his
imminent decomposition or from the moonlight, I could not tell.

I had not said the prayers over my parents' bodies. Ismene had
done that. It was, of course, women's work. Usher in life, usher
in death. But I found I had the words memorized anyway.

Thump, thump.

I mouthed them over my brother. We did not beg for things
in prayers—that was for Followers of Lazarus. Ours were a list
of demands. *Make his rest easy. Weave his soul into his body,
to be preserved and renewed. Keep the best of him and let the
worst slip away.*

I had to hurry, but I felt like I was moving through water
as I pulled the Extractor from beneath my jacket. I wrapped
both hands around it. A shout rang out across the courtyard.
Someone charged toward me. I pressed a button in the side
of the Extractor, and a needle extended from the bottom of
it, so it looked like a giant syringe. I held it over my brother's
stomach.

A strong hand wrapped around my wrist and wrenched it
back. I swung with my other hand, the needle held out like a

weapon. The guard who had stopped me twisted my arm behind my back, and I saw stars. The Extractor fell to the ground next to Polyneikes. I found myself begging.

"Please," I said. "He's my brother. Please."

"Sorry," he said in my ear as he dragged me away.

10

Antigone

"If you were a man," Polyneikes had asked me once, "what would you be?"

The question had annoyed me at the time. We had been sitting on the front steps of our parents' house, teenagers, passing a lit cigarette back and forth. None of our cigarettes were tobacco, anymore—tobacco wasn't useful for food, so it wasn't worth growing. Instead we smoked corn silk rolled in flimsy paper. It was nothing but an idle activity, something to do with your hands while you talked.

I had replied, smoke spilling out of my mouth, "Someone whose gifts aren't wasted for no reason."

I didn't want to change my body. I liked the rhythm that it gave to my life, rising and falling, swelling and shrinking, aching and releasing, with every cycle of the moon. And though I knew there were some men—the state didn't call them that, but my mother had—who could still bear children, I wasn't one of them, either. *People know themselves,* my mother said. *Not fully, not ever, but they know enough.* She was right. I didn't long to be a man. What I longed for, instead, was the freedom to follow my inclinations. The first time Polyneikes went to a meeting of rebels, sneaking out of the house in the early hours of the morning, I was angry that I couldn't go with him. I knew my value. I knew my strengths. The rebellion would be better off if I joined them, too. My absence was to their detriment.

But the womb that gave my life its ebbs and flows made my body sacred to the state, and therefore particularly subject to its might. My mother called this nonsense. She said that protecting a thing was just an excuse to control it. She dedicated herself to freeing people from that control. *Technology can be used for liberty as well as domination,* she wrote, when she petitioned the state to allow her to develop the artificial womb. *Let me prove it to you.*

That was how my parents met.

My mother had been able to make a place for herself in a world that refused to give her one, because she was simply too brilliant to ignore. Because of her genius, she was allowed to occupy spaces that no other woman could. It was the great disappointment of my life that I was not excellent enough to do the same.

I was to be protected, Polyneikes said when I complained of the waste of my gifts. It was the first time since we were children that I shoved him. I couldn't think of anything else to do.

Locked in my bedroom now, waiting for dawn, I realized that all that protection had been for naught. Kreon had ordered execution for anyone who tampered with Polyneikes' body, who tried to collect his ichor. So what good had it done, to guard my womb? I would die anyway. My body was forfeit.

I chewed my fingernails and watched the sky lighten.

Did it have to be?

My mother was a scientist. When my first cycle began, at the age of thirteen, she explained every part of it to me, how my organs knew the steps of an intricate dance, the same one they had been doing for all of human history. I had cried, because I knew something would change—something I had not then been able to articulate, that the world would treat me as a woman then, instead of as a sexless and genderless being of endless potential. I would become subject to a household, guarded by men. She had wiped my tears and told me that plenty of power was still within my grasp, but I would have to learn to wield it, and wielding it was an art. *There are always ways,* she said, *to get your way.* Easy for her to say, I remarked at the time. Not everyone was like her.

But perhaps she was right.

Could my body not have one final purpose?

My body, the same body that Polyneikes had denied my usefulness to protect, the same body that made my consciousness unimportant to rebels—it would outrage them, to see it sacrificed so carelessly, and all for the crime of loving a brother.

I could become something greater than my body simply by allowing myself to use it.

I felt time slow after that. I filled the bathtub and it took an age to undress, the fabric chafing my skin as I peeled it away. I sat in the lukewarm water for too long, as the sun slanted over the ivy outside. I put on a black dress, my funeral clothes. When the lock turned, I was ready.

Flanked by two of Polyneikes' least favorite guards, I walked to Kreon's study. I passed Ismene on the way, taking her morning tea with Eurydice, and didn't spare her a glance. In truth I wasn't sure I could bear to see her expression, whether full of apology that I would not accept or, worse, empty of it.

Kreon's study was on the second floor, overlooking the courtyard. The door was closed. One of the guards knocked for me, and I stared at the wood as I waited for it to open, polished as a mirror. I had been here only once before, when he had summoned me to inform me of my engagement. It was the only place in the city that was not dusty.

Kreon's assistant, the worm Flavian, opened the door for me and gave me an imperious look. In truth, I wasn't sure Flavian had any other kind of look. I moved past him and into the room. The tile floor had been freshly swept; it didn't have the gritty feeling of the stone in the hallway. Two bookshelves framed Kreon's wide desk, made of the same polished wood as the door. He sat with his body angled toward the window and didn't stir. It was as if I hadn't entered.

The worst part about him was seeing my father in him. I wished that I couldn't. They didn't share genes, but he had Oedipus's gestures, surprisingly delicate for a man so prone to brutality. Sometimes he even sounded like my father—the intonation on certain words, the soft way he said goodbye to Eurydice.

But there was an artifice in him that was never in my father. He knew I was standing there. That he chose not to acknowledge me right away was a power play.

Sitting in one of the two chairs opposite him was a guard, wearing his uniform. He looked like every other guard I had ever seen, tall and broad and masculine, his eyes finding me with a level of focus that made me feel shifty and strange. After a moment I recognized him as the guard who had arrested me.

I sat in the chair beside him and waited.

"I wish to hear your account first," Kreon said, and he nodded to the guard beside me.

"Uh . . ." The guard looked from Kreon to me. "After the explosion, everyone vacated the square—I was running there like everybody else, you know, to help with whatever was going on—I wasn't even on duty last night, I was just, you know, trying to do what needed to be done—"

"Get to the point, soldier," Kreon said.

"Well, as I was running past the square I noticed there were no guards, and then I saw something moving, and at first I thought, you know, the body maybe wasn't as *bodylike* as everybody thought, somehow—but then I saw the girl."

"The girl."

"Her." The guard nodded at me.

"You saw her," Kreon said, "doing *what*?"

"Well, she was sort of leaning over him—the body, that is, so I guess I mean she was leaning over *it*—and she was holding something."

"Something."

"An Extractor—one of the older ones, big and clunky, long needle at one end—"

"You're certain of this?"

"Well . . ." The guard shifted a little. "I mean, you can ask her."

"I intend to," Kreon said. "First, however, I would like to know exactly what you saw, in the dead of night, from across a street."

"Well I saw something silvery—the moon was bright—and I ran toward her, and when I was closer, you know, I saw exactly what it was, and I remembered the rules about that body and so I grabbed her."

"All right," Kreon said. "You are dismissed."

"I wasn't even on duty," the guard said.

"So you've said."

"Okay. I just—I hate to be the bearer of bad news, but I wasn't about to *not* do anything, on account of—"

"You're *dismissed,* soldier."

The guard gulped a little, wiped his palms on his trousers, and stood. He gave me an apologetic look, and then walked out of Kreon's study. Kreon stared at me, one eyebrow raised a little, like he was waiting for me to speak. I met his eyes and waited.

"Niece," he said. "I didn't know you knew about explosives."

"I don't, Uncle."

"So you just happened to be in the square, violating my edict, at the exact moment that someone set off an explosive in the Electran District."

I tilted my head. Smiled.

But before I could make my reply, Haemon opened the door to the study. His eyes went straight to his father, and then he gave me a cold look, as if he had never been my co-conspirator.

"I apologize, I didn't know this meeting was already underway," he said, level as a balanced scale. "I had hoped to speak with you beforehand."

I swallowed down the burning in my throat. Haemon must have been worried that I would become an informant to save my skin. He was here to defend himself, to call me a liar before I got the chance to talk about who set the explosion. I sat up straighter. It was a good thing I wasn't going to marry a man who had no respect for me at all.

"I suppose," Kreon replied, equally cool, "you are here to castigate me for ruining your betrothal?"

Just as Kreon had grown up with Oedipus, Haemon had been brought up under his father's watchful eyes, raised to be a worthy successor. Mimicry of Kreon was in his posture and his manner and his expressions.

"A loyal son doesn't berate his father," Haemon said.

"Indeed," Kreon said. "And so?"

"I came to ask you what you intend to do."

"You don't already know?" Kreon looked at me again. "A traitor attempted to kill me. He came close to succeeding. And so I made an example of him. I made an edict, and I made it publicly. In it, I outlined particular consequences for aligning yourself with traitors. Sparing her those consequences would make me a liar."

"And it's better to be an honest man than a merciful one?"
Kreon's voice was like flint when he replied.

"Let me explain something to you, because you are too young
to know it yet." He folded his hands on the desk and leaned toward
me, toward his son. "This city is my household. I am the head of
it. It is a house of people constantly on the edge of starvation,
who begin to deteriorate from the moment they are born. If I
intend to protect them, I do not have the luxury of indulging
defiance. Defiance leads to instability, and instability leads to
extinction. I have built a strong wall around this house. It is not
made of stone, it is made of rules that mitigate damage, and it
has been the great work of my life. What do you think would
happen, if I allowed a crack in my wall?" He looked at me. "Let
me tell you what would happen, because it has happened before,
again and again, reaching back through history: the crack will
widen and the wall will crumble. And when it does, people will
die."

"I see." Haemon sat down in the chair next to mine, where
my friend the guard had sat just a few minutes before. He folded
his hands—he had long fingers, I noticed—over one of his knees.
"As you said, I am too young to know all that you know. But I
have been in the city, and I know how our people think. They will
see this as a senseless killing—the waste of a precious resource, all
for the crime of loving a brother—"

"For the crime of conspiring with rebels," Kreon interrupted.
"Do you think that explosion was a coincidence? It's a wonder
no one was killed."

Haemon went on as if his father had not spoken: "You don't
want to allow a crack in your wall—but the crack is already
there, and I fear this will widen it."

Kreon smirked.

"I see," he said. "You pretend to reason with me, but reason is the furthest thing from your mind. You've developed a hunger for this woman."

"I assure you, my concern is for *you*."

"If your concern was for me, you would be outraged at the attempt on my life by a member of my own household!" Kreon spat. "Instead you are a child, with a child's sense of justice."

"I'm telling you it doesn't matter if I am a child or not, it doesn't matter if I want her or not, it doesn't matter if she *conspired with rebels* or not!" Haemon said. "If the rest of this city agrees with me, you'll bring about the chaos you are trying to avoid."

"I'm not going to capitulate to anyone's tantrums, least of all yours."

Haemon spat, "You're a fool."

"And you're a simpering milksop who is mastered by a woman," Kreon replied. "I do not tolerate murderers and traitors. I will not be persuaded to do so."

The men glared at each other, finally falling into silence. I sat forward and cleared my throat, drawing their attention.

"High Commander," I said. "In the presence of this witness, I'd like to formally call upon the rights of the accused. I want to request a public hearing."

"What?" Haemon said.

Kreon frowned at me.

"It is my right," I said. "To be judged in the presence of my peers."

"This is ridiculous," Haemon said. "There should be no hearing, there should be no judgment in the first place!"

But both Kreon and I ignored him, our eyes locked together like two swords crossed at the blade.

"What do you think you will gain?" he said quietly. His voice was like poison dripping down my throat. "Do you think that if there is some kind of public outcry, I will be moved to change my mind? Well I warn you, girl, I am not so easily swayed."

I pursed my lips, as if to say *we'll see,* but really, I had no doubt: Kreon was a stubborn ass, and that's what I was counting on.

11

Kreon

The statute to which my traitorous niece referred had been proposed by her own father, years before, in response to a particular tendency of the government—then not under my command; that came later—to simply disappear dissenting voices, here one day and gone the next. I remembered the day he had advocated for it before the array of men in jackets buttoned up to their throats, his voice unfaltering, never intimidated even when he ought to have been. It was not confidence so much as a belief in his own invincibility. He never did understand survival—his own, or his children's. He might not have cursed them with his unstable DNA if he had.

Nevertheless, it was not unfathomable that she should remember that statute, as she remembered so many of her parents' *achievements* and routinely reminded me of them. What was startling, then, was not her talent for recall, but her willingness to engage in a public hearing that could only run counter to her best interests. She had been caught with an Extractor in hand, the needle end poised over her twin brother's belly. She had been wrestled away from said body and taken back to her bedroom, where she had been contained since the crime occurred. She could not very well stand before me in the public square and deny any of it.

And besides—what would she have Extracted? There was no soul in Polyneikes' cells. I had permitted the charade for Eteocles, but it was all utterly pointless. There could be no resurrection where there was no pattern to convey.

I had expected her to come trembling to my office, to perch at the edge of the chair and beg me for her life. Despite the ornery streak that ran through her, I knew her to be a practical person above all else. When she had first arrived in this house, I had seen quite plainly the hatred she bore me, yet she had thanked me for my mercy and given me a curtsy that any high-status lady of society would have found acceptable.

So how to account for her attitude in my office? Perhaps she was overconfident in the public's favor and in my unwillingness to be momentarily unpopular. Perhaps her view of things was simply too narrow to account for anything other than her own particular situation. She did not understand the intricacies of leadership, and how could she have? Her life, up until this point, had been one of clinging to the branch until the fruit was ripe enough to pick. One only saw one perspective when dangling for so long.

I scheduled the public hearing for that afternoon, to be announced in the square between the house and the Trireme, according to the requirements of my brother's statute. I doubted that anyone would heed it. I returned to my study, where a cup of coffee waited, lukewarm now thanks to the deviation in my routine. Rather than summon one of the staff to warm it, I clutched it in both hands to preserve the last of its warmth and sipped it at my desk.

Eurydice joined me for lunch, as she often did, setting up plates and napkins at the table on the balcony. Today she put a bud vase between the plates with a paper flower in it, folded dozens of times to make geometric petals. It was red, and her dress was red, too. There was a fragility to her that was on display for all to see, but I was the one who saw her strength. Her calloused hands, from working the ground. Her flat feet, from running barefoot as a child. The scars on her knuckles, from bearing the blows of a cruel teacher's ruler.

When we were sitting across from each other at the table, she said, "About Antigone."

"I don't wish to speak of her again," I replied. "What she did weighs on my mind already."

"Only remember that she is our niece, and she is just a girl," she said softly.

"She is not a girl, she is an adult." I set my jaw. "And as to her relationship to me, well, her brother was just as closely tied to me, and see what *he* tried to do. See what he *did*, firing a bullet into his own flesh and blood!"

My hands shook. I gripped the edge of the table, and looked down at the courtyard where I had seen Eteocles' body. A shameful waste, I had thought even then. Eteocles was not, perhaps, as strong of mind and heart as my own son—not a leader of men, that much was clear. But he had been a thoughtful and capable assistant to me, quick to heed my words and eager to please. And such a thing was not easy to come by.

I had disposed of his ichor after allowing his sister to Extract it. There was no point in storing it. But Ismene was a gentle girl, incapable of the kind of vitriol that readily spilled from the mouth of her sister, and Eurydice had wished to placate her after her sister's violent reaction to the sight of the bodies. She claimed Ismene would be easier to manage if she was not inflamed to rage like her sister. I resented having to manage them at all. Long had I been held hostage by their impurity, and now my house had been riven in two by deception, with my son straddling the divide as if he could keep the land from parting just by wishing it.

Eurydice laid a hand over my own.

"You will do what's right," she said to me. "I know it. I'll go to the hearing, if you want me to."

"Yes," I said. "I could use someone there who will support me."

"Of course."

As she was so skilled in doing, she turned the talk elsewhere, to the garden, to her friends' chatter, to the gossip from the household staff, to anything but what mattered. And I was glad of it.

I heard the crowd that had gathered in the square before I saw it, the murmur penetrating the walls of my house. As I walked with Nikias at my heels through the courtyard, I almost felt the heat of them. I had never been fond of crowds. The mass of humanity only reminded me of how senseless we were, playing games of maturity and civilization when really we were no different than a flock of birds moving as one, each one reacting to the movements of the one in front of it. I had seen more than one riot start because of a stray impulse.

I saw the shadow of my niece in the hallway adjoining the courtyard, smaller than the soldiers that surrounded her. She would enter after me.

I waved to the guards at the gate that separated the courtyard from the street, and they opened it. Dust swirled across the hard-packed earth, a haze appearing between me and my public. My shoulders back, I strode forward. The street was clear now of my traitor nephew's body, removed to the safe room beneath the house after my traitor niece's arrest, so the only thing between me and the crowd was a line of soldiers with staffs in hand. It may as well have been a wall; no one dared breach the invisible line that kept us apart.

I didn't delay. "We are here assembled for a public hearing, in accordance with our statutes, of a woman accused of treason: my niece, Antigone. Lest I be accused of showing favoritism to my own kin, I present my judgment in this matter before all those gathered here. Bring her forward."

She emerged from the courtyard framed with ivy. Her hair was loose and long, and I had not seen it so for months. It made her face look rounder, younger. She had changed clothes—she was still in black, but her shoulders were bare now, and there were faint ripples next to her sternum where her ribs were beginning to show. She was spare, though we had not suffered a food shortage in years, thanks to my rule. Distribution was now strictly controlled, each person given a particular allocation according to their work output, an elegant calculation of calories burned and calories consumed.

Today, her spareness spoke to her fragility. *I am just a child,* her appearance seemed to say, and I was certain this was purposeful on her part. As she had stood before her closet, sorting through black frocks, she had chosen this one for a reason.

I turned away from the crowd—not to hide my face from them, but to position myself as one of them. The head of the flock, the leader of the masses, standing against this woman who had stood against me. It would not hurt to remind them that I was one of them, that I spoke on their behalf and not my own. The crime she had committed was against their survival.

"Antigone," I said. "Do you stand here of your own free will, ready to be questioned?"

"I do," she replied, her voice even.

"Then let me recount the circumstances under which you find yourself accused of treason," I said. "Two nights ago, a group of terrorists stormed the courtyard of this house"—here

I gestured to the building—"with the express intent of doing violence to me and my household. In that attack, your eldest brother, Eteocles, rose up in my defense. He was murdered by one of the aforementioned terrorists, but not before delivering a killing blow to the very man who killed him. That terrorist's name was Polyneikes, and was his brother, and yours, as well as my own nephew."

Her face was impassive. I had always had trouble reading Antigone; it had plagued me since her arrival in my house. I knew that she hated me, yes, but I was never certain of what she would do with that hatred, of whether it would simply fester inside her all her life, or whether it would inspire her to action. Even now, I was not sure of it.

"An attempt on the High Commander's life cannot be tolerated, and is among our highest crimes," I said. "Therefore I delivered an edict, clearly and in the hearing of every citizen of this city: the traitor's body must not be interfered with, under penalty of execution. Did you hear this edict, Antigone?"

"I did," she replied.

"Last night, you were discovered by one of my soldiers immediately following an explosion that caused irreparable damage to the Electran District of our city, including several homes, with an Extractor poised over the traitor's abdomen, in the process of violating my edict. Do you deny it?"

"No, I do not," she said, and a gasp sounded from behind me.

"Do you know who is responsible for the explosion that empowered you to act?"

"I take responsibility for it myself," she replied.

I felt my mouth twist against my will. That was a sidestep if I'd ever heard one. She had obviously conspired with someone, and I was willing to bet it was the same rebels who had stormed the courtyard with her brother. Where one twin had connections, so did the other.

"Was there something about my edict you did not understand?"

"There was plenty about your edict I did not understand," she replied.

"Do elaborate. Was it the definition of 'interference' with the body?"

"No. Your intent was quite clear to me," she said. "You wished to exclude my brother's ichor from the Archive, the only retroactive punishment available to you."

I scowled at her. "What then did you find so confusing?"

"I suppose," she said, "it was the hierarchy of law."

"I beg your pardon?"

"To my knowledge, we have never excluded anyone from the Archive," she said. "Not thieves, not murderers, and not even the rioters who rose up in the wake of a free election gone awry, ten years ago. We even permit those conceived as my siblings and I were to store their ichor, though some doubt it is ichor at all." Her eyes softened. "And so I suppose what confused me was that the merciful approach we have taken toward our wayward citizens prior to this point was suddenly not permitted for my brother."

I breathed deep through my nose. I could not lose control now.

"I should think the explanation for that is obvious," I said. "A thief, a murderer, and even a rioter are not the same as an assassin who acts against the highest level of authority. Such an act is worthy of a stronger punishment. It threatens the very foundation of our society, and our society is our survival."

"My brother was no assassin," she replied.

"Because he was stopped," I said. "By your own brother, no less. I didn't realize you loved Eteocles so little."

"I loved both of my brothers."

"And they killed each other," I said. "It's clear you loved one more than the other, if there was only one whose ichor you risked your life to preserve. Have you given a thought for Eteo-cles' immortality? Do you even know where his body is?"

Her eyes hardened.

"I assumed that you would treat it with respect, given how loyal he was to you," she replied. "Do you think you honor him, by destroying his kin permanently?"

"Do you believe a victim of murder feels warmly toward his murderer?"

"My point," she said, harder now in voice as well as expression, "is that one man, High Commander or no, doesn't have the right or the power to declare cruelty to be morality just because something has affected him personally. There is a word for the man who tries. Do you know what it is, Kreon?" She raised her voice so it rang through the square. "Tyrant."

All around us was silence.

"It is unfortunate to see you this way, Niece," I said, as softly as I could manage.

"In what way?" she said. "Grieving?"

"No," I answered. "Warped beyond recognition. We all knew, of course, that it would happen eventually. Genetic deterioration is the lot of everyone who still lives on this planet. But most people start with a clean slate. You, however . . . un-souled, natural-born daughter of two broken parents . . ." I shook my head. "I am surprised you still trust your own assessments of what is right. Your twin brother did, and it led to him dying in disgrace."

The mask that she had worn up until that point fell away. I had laid bare her hatred, at last.

"If I had a brother who was 'warped,' as you say," she said, "it was Eteocles, who served a power-mad dictator at the expense of his own family."

"Yes, well," I said. "Some of us understand the necessity of duty over personal attachment. And that is why I cannot spare you, dear niece, after hearing you admit to your crimes, as well as your obvious awareness of them, brazenly and in the public square. You cannot be given special treatment simply because of my familial attachment to you. You must suffer the same consequences as every other citizen of this city. You must be executed."

The clamor that rose among the crowd in response to this was deafening. Not just murmurs, but shouts; the soldiers who guarded the square used their staffs to press people back, holding a barrier that had been invisible and was now made manifest.

"You can't!" Ismene emerged from the shadow of the court-yard, followed closely by Eurydice, who reached for her. Ismene tugged away from Eurydice's hand holding her elbow, but not hard enough to break free. Together they stumbled into the square to stand between me and my traitorous niece, Eurydice at Ismene's back.

Tears stained my other niece's cheeks. She was taller than her sister, but softer, her voice gentler. I had wished, many times, that I had selected her to marry Haemon instead of her elder sister. She was easier to deal with.

"You can't," Ismene said again. "I tie my fate to hers. If she dies, so will I, and then two losses will be on your conscience instead of one."

"Ismene!" Antigone shouted the name so that it could be heard over the tumult in the crowd, and scowled at her. "This has nothing to do with you."

"Neither loss weighs on my conscience," I said to Ismene, "when the deaths are the deaths of traitors."

Eurydice spoke softly in the girl's ear, her hands on her shoulders, soothing, pressing her back toward the courtyard. I thought the disruption had been dealt with until my wife left Ismene's side and stepped closer to me, close enough that I could see dust gathering in the creases beneath her eyes.

"Mercy," she said to me softly, "is as fine a quality to be known for as strength, Kreon. Do not sacrifice so valuable a treasure as a young woman's body—not when it has not had time to contribute anything yet."

"What could she contribute, with her origins?" I said, and I flinched as the shouts around us grew louder.

Eurydice's eyes were insistent. *"Life."*

I felt something crawling up my spine—a feeling from memory, soon followed by the images of memory themselves. A man breaking through a barrier, stabbing a soldier. Screams. Chaos. Blood spattering the street. The riot that had almost claimed my life; that *had* claimed the lives of my brother and his wife, and so many others.

I could not allow it to happen again.

I turned toward the crowd.

"Make no mistake, this is not about mercy. Mercy would be valuing the lives of our citizens over the lives of two women!" I gritted my teeth until they squeaked, and then continued: "Still, I am not hard-hearted. I hear you—all of you."

The crowd quieted a little. I turned back to Antigone, standing alone even now, her sister weeping behind her, my wife turning her face away.

"I will not execute her," I said. "But a traitor cannot be permitted to live freely among us. It is too great a threat to our society's health. Instead, I will send her on a special mission. She will board the Trireme, and take our desperate plea into space."

The *and die there* was implied, but I didn't say it aloud.

Our eyes locked. Hers were wide and soft as a rabbit's. She looked up and out toward the ship that glinted in the daylight not far from here, its nose pointed at the heavens.

"Thank you, Niece, for giving us this great gift," I said. "Your last few years will be spent making amends for your treachery. You will be our messenger."

The crowd's quiet had been just a held breath. Their shouts filled the air again, and Nikias rushed forward to escort me back into the courtyard, to be locked safely behind the gates of my house.

12

Antigone

I had seen the true color of the day sky only a few times in my life. The city was shrouded, always, by dust and pollution. On clear days, it was gray-white. On days when the northern wind blew, it was yellow.

But right after a particularly bad storm, when the wind was right, the clouds sometimes cleared, and there it was: blue.

In a world that left no room for the frivolous, it felt almost indulgent. The heavens mocking us, perhaps. But everyone walked around on those days with their heads tilted back, until the wind blew the clouds back into place.

Never did the Trireme glint more. There had been rumors, a few years ago, that the Trireme didn't actually work—why hadn't they launched it yet, if it did?—but that Kreon kept it there to inspire hope for the future. I had halfway believed them, until now, when I knew the Trireme would be my tomb. Kreon wouldn't have given me that sentence if he hadn't known he could carry it out.

I lay on the bed, my fingers spread wide. I felt numb, and the numbness was weight in my limbs. The ceiling, cracked and stained, held no interest, but neither did the dinner they had delivered to me an hour ago. It waited on my desk, cold now. Would they poison me? I didn't think so. Kreon wanted the big, marvelous display of launching me into the sky as much as I did. We just wanted it for different reasons. He was betting it would be a spectacular display of his authority. I was betting it would rouse people to rebellion.

Regardless of who was right, I would still die.

I sat up at the knock. I was certain they wouldn't let Ismene visit me. And anyone Kreon sent would not bother to knock.

The door opened, and Haemon stepped into my bedroom for the second time in two days.

There was trouble in his eyes and a slump to his shoulders. I got up, standing by the foot of my bed, and I meant to say something sour and funny, the way I usually would, but my words failed me, for the first time.

He was at the edges of so many of my memories, after my parents' deaths, but never in the center of them. I suspected he never wanted to intrude on my time with my siblings, certain he wouldn't be welcome, thanks to his father. He had been right about that. We would not have welcomed him.

But a year ago Kreon had summoned me to his study, and Haemon had been there already, sitting with his back so straight it looked painful. Kreon had introduced us to each other as future husband and wife. I had been waiting for him to marry me off—I was not foolish enough to believe that the choice would be mine; soul or not, I was still highborn—and so I received the news in silence. But Haemon had laughed, sharply. I had avoided him since then.

He looked me over, almost like he was checking me for injuries. Only—then his eyes lingered, here on my hip, there on my collarbone.

"I came to break a law," he said.

"I'm not interested in a daring escape," I said.

"Yeah, I realize that," he said. "You think I don't see that you're walking a path you chose?"

I did think that, in fact. But it was becoming clear that I didn't really understand Haemon, didn't really know him. I sat on the edge of my bed, and he moved to stand in front of me. He took a silver Extractor from his back pocket.

It was smaller than the one I had used to try to save Polyneikes. A newer version of the technology. Slim enough to look small in Haemon's hand. He pressed a button on its side, and a needle extended from it.

"You can't Extract ichor from the living," I said.

"I can," he said. "Do you know the history of Extraction? Initially, when the practice began, it was only tied together with our death customs because it took so long to edit the genes affected by the virus. But this notion that the soul in our cells can only be Extracted properly after death, that came later."

"You think if you take my cells now, you'll take my soul with them?" I asked, and I wanted to laugh, but there was no laughter in me.

Haemon shook his head. He cradled the Extractor in both hands.

"Suppose," he said. "Suppose I think the soul is an eternal, ever-regenerating thing. That your soul can be simultaneously whole in you and whole in your ichor—suppose I think that it's possible it suffuses every part of you, powerful and potent. Suppose that even if I am not certain of this, I am willing to risk it to preserve you."

He held the Extractor out to me, and I felt a momentary pain—if he had convinced Pol of this, I could have stored Pol's ichor while he was still alive—but I pushed it aside. It was too late for that now.

I shook my head, pushing the Extractor away.

"Speak to the mystics," I said. "Ask them if I even have a soul."

"Don't be stupid," he said. "I don't need to ask. I already know."

I shook my head again.

"I don't care about the law," he said, and he sank to his knees in front of me. Kneeling, he was almost as tall as I was sitting on my low bed. We were eye to eye, and the Extractor was between us. "What my father is doing is wrong, and only something wrong can make it even a little bit right again."

"No, it's not . . . it's not that," I said. "It's a kind gesture, Haemon, but I don't want to be stored in the Archive at all."

His eyes were hard and fixed.

"I don't believe in immortality," I said. "I think you could use an ovum from my body—you could bring back the shape of me, refined and edited, but you could never bring *me* back. And an edited version of me is not me anyway."

"But Pol—"

"Pol did believe in it," I said. "The last thing he asked me to do was to use that Extractor. So I did my best." I shrugged. "Look at what came of that."

The sky was getting dark. I had read somewhere once that in the dark, our eyes relied more on rods than on cones, meaning that night vision and color vision were incompatible. So I always thought of sunset as the color draining out of the world, like dye leeching out of a garment when you rinsed it. The little courtyard beyond my bedroom window was turning gray.

And then I couldn't see even that, through tears.

"Sorry," I said, choking.

Haemon put the Extractor down and took my hands in his.

"Don't be," he said. "I can go, if you'd like. But I thought maybe you'd prefer even my company to being alone."

"Even yours." I laughed a little. "If you knew what I was thinking about, you'd know why that was funny."

"You could always tell me. Maybe I'll laugh."

I squeezed my eyes shut.

"I was thinking about all the things I won't do," I said. "Won't have a wedding. Won't walk through the Archive. Won't get crow's feet." I laughed again, and my laugh broke. "I didn't want to be married, but I thought I would *get* married. I thought Ismene would put flowers in my hair, and I would wear my mother's dress, and I would have a wedding night and wake up and decide whether I felt any different. I didn't want children, either, but I thought I would have them—thought I would walk through the Archive and find someone who looked like my mother, and make the best of the thing I didn't want. I thought I would find the moments I loved among the moments I didn't. I thought I would have *time*."

His hands tightened around mine. His hands were warm and I focused on that, the heat in his fingers, the heat behind my eyes, the blood and muscle of him, of me, the life in us both. Technically, there would be life in me for years yet. There were as many rations on the Trireme as the ship could hold, so it could broadcast from as far away from Earth as possible. And that was the worst part of it, that I would have to choose between taking my own life—driven mad by the isolation—and watching my food supply dwindle. That I would be both alive and dead at the same time for so long, cursed to hover between the two, unobserved.

"This morning it felt so easy to give all that away," I said. "Pol, he was worried I wanted to die. Ismene, too. But I didn't, I don't. I just wanted to be done, and that's not the same thing."

"I know," he said softly. "I know it's not."

I had imagined marriage as a cage. Even my mother, in love with my father as she was, hadn't been able to escape that. People asking my father how he allowed my mother so much autonomy, as if he was her jailer. The way men wouldn't listen to her unless he repeated what she said. And love was never going to be mine to claim, so I had imagined worse than that—an arrangement of restriction and demand. But I had never imagined Haemon, specifically. Thoughtful Haemon with his watchful eyes. Big and strong enough to be capable of violence, but I had never once seen him inclined toward it.

"You helped me," I said. "We could have gotten married sooner, if I hadn't delayed. We could have had good things together, I think. And now I'll never have any of them."

"I know," he said again. My mother had always yelled at me for saying that, *I know,* even when I didn't, just because I was annoyed with her for nagging at me. He didn't say it like that. He said it more like an acknowledgment, heard and then understood. I wondered if he had thought about our marriage, what it would be like, how our children would be, what we might choose. A life after Kreon's death. I could have asked. But I thought it might be worse to hear the answer.

"There are still good things you could have," he said. "You need only ask."

I opened my eyes. He was still on his knees—like a supplicant, his words a kind of offer.

I thought of his hands on me, and I wanted it.

I bent my head toward his, and our lips touched, just for a moment, like palms pressing together. It was like a test—is this all right, is this the kind of madness that makes a certain amount of sense. I decided it was, and I kissed him again, slowly this time, and though his mouth was spare and though I hardly knew him, it felt how I imagined it was supposed to feel, warm and lively as an exposed wire.

I pulled him toward me and we fell back against my bed, and I stripped him bare and I took my time looking at him and I took, and I took, and so did he. And there was no pain, only strangeness, and for a few hours more, at least, I was alive.

It was strange to sleep on the eve of banishment. In the moments before I drifted off, I thought that I should have been drinking in everything that I could, everything that I loved about this planet. It was not a lovable place in so many respects, but its gravity steadied me, its sky enfolded me, its scents instructed me, and none of those things would accompany me into the Trireme. But my body was still a body, and it still needed sleep.

I fell asleep with my head on Haemon's shoulder, my arm slung around his waist. He was so warm I didn't need the sheet that covered me. He didn't snore, exactly, but his breaths were loud and slow when he slept. When I woke a few hours later, his fingers were still laid across my rib cage, but the loud, slow breathing had turned quiet. He was awake.

I lifted my head and looked at him.

Despite the fact that we were naked—despite the fact of what we had done together—it was still odd to be so close to him. I had spent the last year avoiding him, and all the years before that not seeing him at all.

"I can't let this happen to you," he said to me.

"I chose this," I said. "The moment I requested a public hearing, I knew what would come of it."

"You shouldn't have to choose it," he said. "I *won't* let this happen to you. I have to do something."

He sat up, wrapping his arms loosely around his knees, bent under the sheet. I stood, and walked to the window. Goose bumps spread over my skin from the cold, now that I was no longer lying against him. The moon was shrouded in clouds.

"Your attachment to me will fade," I said.

"I have been *attached* to you for a long time," he said sharply.

I looked back at him. I really couldn't read Haemon at all, could I? He was at the edges of so many of my memories—but maybe he had put himself there so that he could still be in them at all. He had come for me after Polyneikes died, to see if I was all right. He had waited for me in the courtyard. He had rigged an explosion—or gotten someone else to do it—as a distraction. He had tried to shout down his father.

His eyes skimmed my bare body, and a small voice in my head told me that if he cared for me, it was an advantage I could not ignore. My gut twisted at the thought.

"Let it go, Haemon," I said.

"That is an absurd thing to say," he replied. "I am not going to just stand back and watch you die."

And he wouldn't, of course. Like the path that was leading me to the Trireme, Haemon's course was already set. Neither of us could change it now.

"Fine," I said. "Then there's someone you should meet, and I can tell you where to find him."

13

Haemon

The symbol for the North District, where I found myself in the early hours of the morning, is the sphinx. Head of a woman, body of a lion, wings of a bird. *Best of all worlds,* Mom liked to say; *everybody should be so lucky.* Sphinxes were known for being merciless as well as tricky, tellers of riddles and killers of men, and I'd found that the symbols for the districts reflected their personalities—or maybe the personalities had grown around the symbols.

Either way—I knew to be wary of the North District. I was the High Commander's son, after all. So I went with a knife at my hip and my eyes open. I took the path she'd told me to take, which sidestepped the worst parts. It carried me down narrow alleys with laundry hanging overhead, around sharp bends with bulging mirrors attached to the corners of buildings so you could see who was coming the other way, under wires that dipped too low so neighbors could share electricity illegally. Everything smelled either like trash or like stew, and the worst was when you got a whiff of both at once.

I ended up at Parthenopaeus's house, a green door with the little pot of pinkish rocks next to it. There were stubs of cornsilk cigarettes among the rocks. I knocked before I could really think about it, and then I thought about it afterward. Knocking here was basically treason. That was how Dad would see it. I could still turn around, probably, without anybody knowing, but I still had this feeling that he would know. He knew more than people thought he did. He was always having people followed, or "disappeared," hence all the monkshood in the greenhouse—great for poisoning someone so nobody would know it. Wasn't hard to poison someone in a city where people died all the time.

Anyway, the door opened. A little old lady stood inside the foyer, her face crumpling in like a collapsed cake, a scarf covering her hair. She stared up at me without speaking.

"I'm here to see Parth," I said. "Antigone sent me."

"That girl's nothing but trouble," she said.

I smiled a little. "I like her just fine."

"Then you're nothing but trouble, either. Come in."

She shuffled away from the door, and I bent my head to step into the house. All I knew about Parth was that he was big and not as stupid as he pretended to be—that was Antigone's description. I wasn't quite ready for all the people in the house—men, all of them, except for the old woman, draped over couches and chairs, or crouched around the coffee table playing a board game I didn't recognize. One of them stood up, and he was big, taller and broader than me, his head shaved.

"Who're you?" he said. I was pretty sure this was Parth.

"Antigone sent me," I said.

"That wasn't what I asked."

"I'm Haemon," I said.

"Kreon's boy?"

"Yes and no," I said.

"What the hell kind of answer is that?"

"There are sons and there are sons." I shrugged. "Whose boy are you?"

He narrowed his eyes at me, and then motioned for me to follow him into the next room. It was hard to find a path across the space—it wasn't a big living room, and there were six people in it, all staring at me like they wanted to burn holes in my skin. I stepped into the kitchen and I was relieved to close the door behind me. Parth had gone right to the sink to wash a plate. He pointed with wet fingers at one of the chairs.

"Sit," he said. "You said Tig sent you?"

"I didn't know anybody but her siblings called her that."

"They don't, I guess," he said. "Thirsty?"

"No, thank you."

He wiped his hands off on a dish towel and turned to face me. He didn't sit down, just leaned against the counter and folded his massive arms.

"Well? What are you here for?"

"Do you know what happened to her yesterday?"

"Heard she got caught trying to suck out Pol's genes," he said.

"And she was sentenced to execution via Trireme."

"As I understand it, the word 'execution' was never used."

My chest tightened.

"She'll spend years alone in space," I said. "And then starve to death up there."

This, at least, seemed to sober him. He looked down at his toes.

"Yeah, I know," he said. "Listen, she was never all that friendly to me, but I wouldn't wish that on her. Or most anyone."

"Well. I don't intend to let it happen."

The faucet was letting out a slow trickle of water that *tap, tap, tap*ped on the bottom of the sink. Parth sized me up.

"How do you mean to stop it?" he said. "What your daddy

wants to happen pretty much does happen, dunno if you've noticed."

"I don't know how to stop it," I said. "That's why I'm here, talking to a rebel leader."

Parth laughed.

"What gives you the idea I'm *that*?"

"She did," I said.

"She's just some girl with busted wiring."

"She said you were a smart guy who tried to look dumb," I said.

He laughed again—deeper this time, like he really meant it. "Smart guys don't commit treason, especially not in front of Kreon's kid."

"Well, I committed treason two nights ago, by setting off an explosion that gave Antigone her opportunity to use an Extractor," I said. "So now you have a weapon against me. Maybe you won't mind so much giving me one against you."

"How would someone like you know how to set off an explosion?"

"I had a rebellious phase as a teenager," I said. "Used to go to East Field, you know that empty lot in the Neïstan? I'd blow things up there. All you need is some fertilizer, and the High Commander's house has plenty."

"Shameful waste of fertilizer."

"Like I said, I was a teenager. Not exactly thinking about conservation of resources at that age."

A shout from the next room punctured our silence. I straightened, sure for a second that my father's men had come to the apartment—but laughter followed, just the board game running its course. Parth waited for it to die down before he spoke.

"Say you could set off another explosion," he said. "How would you time it?"

"There are ways," I said. "The more important question is: time it for what purpose?"

"Do you know how an arch is built, Haemon?" Parth said. He pulled out the seat across from mine. It creaked under his weight. He put the heels of his hands on the table. "You build up the sides, so they curve up, like this." He curved his hands so the heels stayed planted and the fingers arched over them. "And then you stick a rock right here at the middle." He tapped his fingertips together. "We call that rock a cornerstone. It keeps the arch stable, so both sides are balancing against each other. But if you knock out the cornerstone . . ." He slapped the table with both palms. "Wham. Arch comes down. So you can either spend all your time chipping away at the little bricks, or . . ." He looked at me, one eyebrow raised. ". . . you can go straight for the one that really matters. See what I mean?"

I did, of course.

My father was the High Commander of this city. The cornerstone. He was not the only one in power here, but all the others took guidance from him, sought his approval. Without him, everything would fall apart.

"You want me to kill my father," I said.

"Now, I didn't say anything of the kind," Parth said. "But if we were to lose our cornerstone, there are a great deal of people poised to take advantage of the chaos that would follow."

"Opportunists?" I said. "And would any of them be any better than the High Commander?"

"Some better, some worse," he said. "But all committed to a free election."

"And if the election turns out someone worse?"

Parth leaned forward.

"Then at least we would be responsible for our own doom," he said, "instead of someone else deciding it for us. And really, isn't that the most any of us can hope for?"

I wished I had asked for water. My throat was dry and I needed something to do with my hands.

The first time I saw my father's cruelty on full display was during the riots, as he watched my uncle, Oedipus—the first and last victor of a free election this city had had—get struck down by soldiers. He did nothing to stop it; he just watched the man fall. I was only a boy at the time, still half convinced that my dad, a man I was afraid of, might have some good in him.

He never touched me, or my mother, only raised his voice to us a handful of times. But there was always danger in him, boiling just beneath the surface. It made my steps careful and my words guarded. It made me sneak into the kitchens to play poker instead of just going there. He didn't have to shout at me or smack me around for me to know what wasn't going to be acceptable to him. His shadow was long, and filled every corner of our house.

Still, the little boy who wanted to find something behind the fear lived.

Could I kill Kreon?

"How would this save her?" I said.

"She's the figurehead of a resistance movement now," Parth said. "For some reason, you talk to people about food shortages, power outages, contaminated water, the government disappearing people—you might as well be speaking another language. But if you tell them their High Commander wants to send a pretty young thing into space to waste away? Suddenly they're listening."

Parth leaned back and sighed.

"What I'm telling you is," he said, "people all over this goddamn city are itching to keep that ship from launching. You just have to give them an opening."

I thought of the monkshood blooming in our greenhouse, and the curve of Antigone's hip in the moonlight, and the way my father had sneered at me as I argued for mercy. Somehow I didn't feel like I was making a choice. I felt like he had already made all the choices, and I was just the response to his call, the effect of his cause.

"That's what I'll do, then," I said.

14

Antigone

What ought a person wear to go to their tomb?

I opened the doors of my wardrobe and stared. Just an hour ago, an aide from the Trireme office—a dusty, neglected place with a handful of employees, all of them engineers—had come to my door escorted by soldiers to tell me what to expect from the journey. I could pack a bag, he said, as heavy as I wanted, though I knew no one would offer to carry it for me. When he left, I had numbly filled a small sack with underwear and socks, comfortable pants and clean T-shirts, my father's old sweater, my mother's old necklace. I had bathed, meaning to savor the warm water for the last time. But that was the thing about last times—you kept pressing into yourself for a more pure experience, but the pressure made any experience impossible. I barely felt the water.

I stood naked in front of the wardrobe, my skin still drying. Did I feel different, now that I had been seen, known? Now that I had felt yet another thing my body was capable of doing? More than two decades on this Earth and my body still surprised me. Perhaps that was why some people were so eager to have children.

They wanted to test the boundaries of what their bodies could do, enter into a mysterious state that was no less mysterious for being experienced by so many others. I would not feel those things—life stirring inside me, my belly swelling and hardening like an eggshell. I would never feel them. But not all things are guaranteed for all people. That is the way of things.

I took out the box from the bottom of my closet and opened it. Inside was my mother's wedding gown. A simple garment, all things considered, with some beading at the bodice that she had stitched herself—I could tell by how crooked the threads were, when I looked closely. It was white, its brightness only a little faded by time. The fabric was so fine it felt like water in my hands. I shook it out, gently, and then unzipped the back and stepped into it. She was built a little narrower than I was, but also taller. The straps were set a little wider than my shoulders, and the train dragged on the ground by an inch or two, but it fit.

I felt wild, mad, as I twisted my hair up away from my neck. As I dabbed a red stain on my lips, so like blood, and smeared it into my cheeks to make them look flushed. I stood before the mirror, facing away from the room as a servant arrived with my lunch tray.

"Tig."

I had not given the servant a second glance. She was dressed in the usual uniform, her hair pulled back so tight it looked painful. But as I looked at her in the mirror, standing with the tray in her hands, I realized she was Ismene. I turned, heat rushing into my cheeks as she saw me in our mother's wedding gown.

"How did you get in here?" I said.

She set the tray down on my desk and rushed toward me, her hands outstretched. I took them in mine without thinking twice. Her palms were cold and trembling. Her entire body was trembling, her breaths shaking on the way out.

"I bribed the maid with coffee," she said. "The guards didn't recognize me."

No one ever recognized Ismene. There was something about her face—pretty, but forgettable.

"Idiots," I said.

Her eyes dropped to my body, wrapped in fine white fabric, and my feet, bare and dusty on the floor.

"You're wearing Mom's dress."

I cringed, pulling away. "I know. It's stupid. I should leave it here for you—"

"No." She shook her head. "No, you have to wear it. Imagine the look on Kreon's face when he sees you in it."

She turned me around so we were both looking at my reflection in the mirror, her chin just above my shoulder.

"Besides," she said, "I don't intend to marry."

"Nor did I," I said. I gentled my voice. It was different for Ismene than it was even for me, I knew. "We don't always have a choice in the matter."

"No, no, you don't understand." She frowned at me. "I intend to go with you, instead."

"Ismene—"

"I'm sorry I didn't help you," she said, her eyes welling up with tears. "I'm sorry I didn't knit our fates together like I should have. I'm so—"

I pulled her into my arms, fierce, our heads almost colliding. I could feel her jawbone against my cheek, her fragile shoulders under my wrists. Life had made us both spare, even living in Kreon's house. We were very sharp to the touch, knife-edge women.

"It doesn't matter," I said. "Do you think I want you to suffer the same fate as me? I'm so glad you didn't help me, now."

But she shook her head and pulled back from me.

"I don't want to go with you so that I can redeem myself," she said. "I want to go with you so that you won't be alone."

"Your reason makes no difference, I still won't accept."

"My reason makes all the difference," she said firmly. "I am not a miserable sinner wearing sackcloth and dust. I am your sister, who would rather live a few years with you than many years without you. Is that so difficult to understand?"

In that moment, I wanted to accept her offer, and I felt ashamed. I didn't want to die alone in the emptiness of space. I didn't want to see and have no one to share with, to scream and have no one hear me. I didn't want to be the first and the last of us to know what it was like to float among the stars. There was warm temptation in agreeing, like giving in to the desire to fall back into bed on a cold morning. But behind it was the horrible guilt I knew I would feel if I did.

She cupped my face in her hands.

"What are the years worth?" she said in a whisper, her eyes fixed on mine. "Let me tell you a secret, Antigone, something I have never told anyone: I am *glad* the same blood runs in our veins. I'm like a bird that's fallen in love with its own reflection; I am relieved every time I see myself in your face, and our mother, and our father. If I stay here without you, I will never be able to be what I should, I will only wear away at my time, waiting for the end."

She smiled, and I realized my cheeks were wet.

"If I go with you," she said, "we will have a beautiful, brief adventure. So let me give you this. Let me take this from you."

I closed my eyes. My face was hot. I had heard, for just a moment, not Ismene's voice, but the voice of our mother. And I wondered if maybe I was wrong—maybe immortality did exist, if my mother could speak through Ismene. If I could still hear her, even after death.

I couldn't speak. I nodded instead.

15

Eurydice

That morning I looked at Kreon's razor, drying on the edge of the sink, and thought about the day Haemon was implanted in my body. How I had, for an hour, thought about the end. Maybe it was natural to think about death when you were making new life. Maybe it wasn't. Either way, procedure was what carried me through: I simply did what I was supposed to until the urge faded.

The Trireme was set to launch in late morning. It was poised at the edge of a clearing in the distance. The clearing abutted a gentle hill. A crowd waited at the top of that hill, in a bare patch of street hemmed in by buildings, not unlike the one where the whole nasty business had taken place the day before yesterday.

I went to the building that faced the Trireme and climbed up the fire escape to the balcony overlooking the square. I was careful to stand in the shadows where the crowd below couldn't see me. They had already gathered. From a distance, it might have seemed like they were there for a spectacle. People had been gathering to watch executions since time immemorial.

I was sure that's what Kreon would see. Just morbid curiosity, for most. For others, perhaps, pleasure. I knew the oddities

that afflicted our species. Maybe that's why my mother was convinced I was a prophet—because I saw things clearly.

But as close as I was to them, standing on the balcony right
above their heads, I could tell that the people were not here for a
spectacle. They shuffled, restless. Muttered. Pointed as they took
note of the guards positioned at the perimeter of the square. Directly across from me, elevated a foot above the crowd, was a
platform. It stood between the people and the hill that led down
to the Trireme. The guards kept the people from climbing on it;
it was where Kreon and Haemon and I would stand to watch
the ship launch.

The ship was huge. Even though it was a ways off, across the
square, down the hill, it loomed over us all. Bigger than most of
our buildings. I had gone the night before with Kreon to make
sure it was all in order. His instructions up until that point had
been to ensure the Trireme was ready to launch at all times. He
had never known when its launch would be most useful to him.

I had gone to persuade him that now was not the time. He
had been angry with me for contradicting him in public, at the
hearing, but his anger was a cold, lifeless thing. It made him
into stone, and now he wouldn't listen. I knew him, and I knew
I had made him impossible to reach by daring to disagree with
him at that pivotal moment, yet I still had to try. Not just for
our niece Antigone, who I liked well enough, and not just for a
young woman who had wanted to honor her brother—but for
Kreon himself.

This crowd was not gathered for a spectacle.

They were gathered to see if the thing that horrified them
would really come to pass.

And that was not a crowd that would favor Kreon.

"They told me you were up here," Kreon said, his hand finding the small of my back. "What are you looking at, Wife?"

We were a love match. My father was too negligent in his

duties—too lost in moonshine—to arrange a match for me. My mother, hanging on my every word, would simply do as I said. My cousin took me to a party, thrown in an abandoned building in the Neïstan District. In those days people were dying faster than they were being born. A lot of buildings were abandoned. Empty. Crumbling. If we weren't careful, analysts said, we would lose valuable genetic diversity and we would not be able to survive. That was why the compulsory child-bearing regulations began.

But the party—

There weren't many girls there. It wasn't what respectable girls did. But at that time, I was tired of being respectable, so I went. All the boys there were military. It was the only way to look clean-cut—the uniforms were better maintained than most people's hand-me-downs and repurposed old clothing. Kreon was one of the only ones who looked like he needed to shave. His jaw was strong; so was his brow. When he met me, he bowed a little, like I was a queen. The others teased him for it, but I thought it was sweet. There was always something sweet about him in those days. Awkward. Sure of himself in his work, but with me, so careful, like he thought he might break me. It was nice to be taken care of. I had always done the caretaking. After all, I was the prophet of my house. God's Chosen.

Now, I wished Kreon would see me that way, just long enough to correct his mistakes.

"I am looking at trouble brewing," I said to him. One last try.

"They seem peaceful enough."

"They're not," I said sharply, and I glared at him. "For years you have instructed them to value not the minds of people who bear children but their bodies. Now you seek to dispose of one because she cares for her brother—"

"Because she *defied me*—"

"They do not see that part! They see only that you are careless with a precious resource. That you seek obedience without rational thought!"

"Obedience," he said, and he put his hand on my elbow and drew me closer. "Obedience is essential to our survival."

I tensed. In all our years, Kreon had never hurt me, never grabbed me. This was not like him.

"That may be," I said, and I pulled my arm free. "But you cannot force people to see the world your way."

I saw Haemon standing near the platform. He crouched down beside it, so that for a moment I thought he was tying his shoelace. But no—he was looking at something beneath it, something I couldn't see. He straightened, and looked up at the balcony where we stood. I could not read his expression from here. But I saw things clearly; I always had.

"I must go speak with our son," I said.

Walking through the crowd, my suspicions were confirmed. There was a buoyancy to crowds that waited in eager anticipation. It was absent here. The tension here was that of a finger on a trigger, a wire pulled tight enough to snap. A soldier escorted me across the square, but shoulders still bumped me from all angles. Voices chased me all the way to where Haemon stood, waiting for us on the platform. His face was drawn. When he set a hand on my shoulder to steady me as he kissed my cheek, it was shaking. I frowned up at him.

"I don't know what you're doing," I said. "But if it's making you look this sick, I'm sure you don't want to do it."

"My father is about to kill my betrothed," he said. "How else am I supposed to look?"

I was not used to words failing me. But this was an extraordinary situation. I pursed my lips and by that time, Kreon was making his way through the crowd.

He was flanked by soldiers, but the simmer of the crowd reached a boil when he was among them. People edged closer, pressing against the men that protected my husband. One man threw himself at Kreon, and a soldier's retaliation was swift. He brought the butt of his gun down on the side of the man's head. The man collapsed into the crowd, disappearing. Kreon made it to the platform as the crowd roared. I saw the injured man resurface with a red streak of blood on his face.

The shouts were deafening. The soldiers held their weapons crosswise, the rifles becoming a barrier. Kreon's eyes were too wide, the whites showing, as he looked back at the Trireme. He took the radio communicator from his belt and held it up to his mouth. I couldn't hear what he said, but I reached for him. His arm felt like steel beneath my fingers.

Our eyes met.

"If you do this," I said to him, "they will revolt."

The platform beneath the Trireme roared to life. A flame ignited beneath the ship. Smoke curled over its base. At the sight of fire, the crowd erupted. The wall of sound was like a physical thing; it pushed me into Kreon.

"You're right," he said to me.

It was as if my body had turned to water. Weak with relief, I clung to him. I smiled up at him and, for a moment, he appeared to me just as he had all those years ago, awkward and sweet.

It would be all right, it would—

A man broke through the barrier of soldiers and barreled toward us. Kreon turned to shield me, and the radio communicator flew out of his hand. It bounced on the platform and broke in half.

We both stared at it. I dove for the pieces, hoping it was just that the battery had fallen out, but it was split in half at its seam, the parts spread over the platform.

"Mom!" Haemon said. "Mom, you have to get out of here!"

I looked up at Kreon, who was staring with horror at the Trireme. I stood, leaving the radio communicator on the ground, and shoved him toward the edge of the hill. He stumbled off the platform, just barely keeping his balance.

"Go down there!" I shouted. "Go!"

Kreon took off running. I hadn't seen him run like that in a long time. He tumbled down the slope as the crowd broke through the barrier. I heard a gunshot. Haemon grabbed me around the waist and hauled me off the platform, his hand on my head to keep it down. An elbow caught me in the cheek.

"Run!" Haemon screamed.

And then the platform exploded.

The sound—*the sound,* so loud it filled my head and rattled my teeth. The force threw us both forward, into a woman with gray, curly hair and a man wearing a bandana around his head to catch his sweat. Together, Haemon and I tumbled to the ground. Someone fell on top of me, their knees digging into my legs. I hit my head on the pavement, and the spray of shrapnel was sharp, stinging my shoulders and back.

I lifted my head just in time to see a ball of light expanding around the base of the Trireme.

Kreon hadn't made it in time. The ship was launching.

Haemon screamed. I couldn't hear him—everything was muffled—but I saw the anguish in his face, like kindling split by an axe. He stumbled to his feet, over the wreckage, to the edge of the hill. He must have known it was too late to do anything. I tried to go after him, but my legs wouldn't cooperate. A hand closed around my arm, a soldier pulling me up. I recognized him—Nikias, head of Kreon's guard. He spoke to me, and I watched his mouth moving but couldn't make out the words.

I managed to see *Let's go,* and he lifted me to my feet. I looked back to see Haemon swallowed by the raging crowd, and Kreon on the hillside, alone, and the streak of the Trireme in the sky.

For a long time, I was alone.

Nikias carried me like a bride back to the house. By that time, I had recovered enough to walk. I smacked his shoulder to get him to put me down; he wasn't listening to me. I could hear my own voice, though it sounded far away. He led me by the hand to the safe room beneath the house. He sat me down there, on the low cot in the corner, and he gave me water, and checked me for injuries. I meant to thank him, but I wasn't sure if I managed it or not. He left me, promising to get an update.

It felt like a long time before anything changed. My glass of water was empty. My feet were bleeding, and my body ached. The door to the shelter opened, and it wasn't Kreon who walked through it. It was Nikias. His expression was blank. A studied blankness—the face of someone who didn't want to give himself away. I stood, my stomach heavy.

"Which one?" I said, because I knew, I knew that someone was dead, and there were only so many people it could be.

In the moment before he answered, I prayed that it was Kreon. A woman can fall in love more than once, but she cannot replace a child. The thought felt almost brutal to me, but grief lays us bare, even to ourselves. I prayed that my husband was dead, because I knew how that would go: I knew where I would get the Extractor for his ichor, what I would wear to mourn him, how I would process through the streets with my son at my side to the Archive. All women in our city know the procedures for losing a spouse.

But there are no procedures for losing a child.

Which is why, when Nikias hesitated to respond, I felt it as a physical blow to the gut. I stumbled back and sat on the cot. *No,* I thought, and I stood.

"Show me," I said.

Together we climbed the steps to the hallway above. It should have been in chaos, staff rushing everywhere, as it always was during emergencies. Instead it was silent. Everyone we passed avoided my eyes. I followed Nikias to the courtyard.

My son lay on the ground, and I thought of a particular memory. Haemon, age eight, on a clear night, asking me to see the stars. We had gone up to the roof of our building, then an apartment in the Seventh District. The moon had been a crescent— *Like a toenail clipping,* Haemon had said, and I'd laughed. We had lain down side by side on the roof and looked up at the night sky until the clouds blew in again and our noses were cold.

For just a moment, time fractured, and I saw him as that eight-year-old boy lying on the roof. And then time returned, and I knew this was his body, and my boy, my love, my dearest and most precious thing, was dead.

I was still kneeling there at his side when Kreon returned.

It was late afternoon, and I was numb. I couldn't feel my feet or my hands. I couldn't feel pain.

I looked up at the man, my husband, standing grief-stricken in the courtyard.

"Eurydice," he sighed.

I pushed myself to my feet. My vision went black, just for a moment, as the blood rushed back into my extremities. When I saw again, he was reaching for me. I stepped back.

"Look carefully, Kreon," I said, my voice still distant, and rough, as if I'd been screaming. "Because you will never see me again."

At dusk, I carried my son's ichor to the Archive.

And then I kept walking until I was in the wilderness.

16

Antigone

It is, I imagine, a little like the horror of being born.

We come into the world screaming, after all. There is *warm* and *safe,* and then there is motion, and pressure, so intense we can hardly stand it. And then everything is loud and bright and strange, and we can't help but scream at the top of our lungs.

Ismene screams during the launch. I don't blame her. It is a forceful, helpless feeling. Like being thrown, like dreams where I am falling and feel terrified of my own weight. Fear washes over me, prickling and stinging, and I grit my teeth against it. Ismene sobs as we break through the clouds. I want to be sobbing, but my body has become a prison, and I can't move.

I watch through the porthole as Earth appears beneath us.

It didn't occur to me until that moment that I had lived inside her. I always thought of my planet as something I lived *on*. But clinging to the straps that hold me in place, I think, no, I was within her. Folded somewhere between her atmosphere and her surface, as if between a mattress and a blanket. But there are depths to her I don't know, and layers I never thought of. She is a complex entity that I know, in the end, very little about. I watch her become distinct from me, and it seems to me that gravity was a kind of umbilical cord that bound us to our planet, and that cord has been cut.

So of course I am afraid. Nothing is more frightening than the sudden realization that you are new.

I reach over to Ismene and grab her hand.

"Here I am," I say, and it's nonsense, just words to fill the space. But it seems to help her.

She turns her hand and interlaces her fingers with mine.

"Here I am," I say again, this time to myself.

Acknowledgments

First of all, you can't write a retelling of *Antigone* without acknowledging Sophocles. Hot damn, what a play. Secondary nods to Euripides and Aeschylus for their supporting material (though Euripides's version of this play is, of course, lost to time). If you haven't read the original, please do.

Thank you to Lindsey Hall for your enthusiasm and wisdom and book-induced despair (but like, in a good way). Joanna Volpe, for always being instantly on board every time I randomly appear in your inbox with new dreams.

Thank you to the entire team at Tor, especially: behind-the-scenes wizardry from Rafal Gibek, Dakota Griffin, Steven Bucsok, Rachel Bass, and Aislyn Fredsall; marketing and publicity pizzazz from Sarah Reidy, Renata Sweeney, and Emily Mlynek; detail-oriented reading from Lauren Hougen, Su Wu, and Lauren Riebs; exterior and interior beauty courtesy of Greg Collins, Katie Klimowicz, and Pablo Hurtado de Mendoza; and captains of various ships Eileen Lawrence, Lucille Rettino, and Devi Pillai.

New Leafers! Jordan Hill, for your support and your keen eye. And of course Meredith Barnes, Emily Berge-Thielmann,

Jenniea Carter, Katherine Curtis, Veronica Grijalva, Victoria Hendersen, Hilary Pecheone, and Pouya Shahbazian for all the work you do on all my books.

Kristin Dwyer, for continuing to crush it, and also, all the Dune GIFs a gal could ask for.

Adele Gregory-Yao, for keeping me on track. Elena Palmer, for your thoughtful feedback.

Nelson, for immediately reading *Antigone* when I slapped it on your desk last year, signaling your willingness to walk with me down all the weird paths.

My family and friends, for always cheering me on.

Robert Bagg, for my very first translation of *Antigone,* and Anne Carson, for the one that reignited my interest.

I've been racking my brains trying to figure out which teacher, specifically, introduced me to this play in high school . . . and I've come up empty. But to them: thank you for fostering my love of it.

And finally, S, for telling me "Write it!" . . . because otherwise I wouldn't have.